DROPPING

ISBN : 0-95

**First Published October 2004 by
SeaNeverDry Publishing
www.seaneverdrypub.com**

Cover artwork by Chrissie Abbott

1

Acknowledgments

I am indebted to Idi Amin for inspiring this
romp
To the Ministry of Overseas Development
who introduced me to East Africa
To Ewen Reekie for his karate advice and
terminology
And especially to Dave Abbott without
whom this book would not have been
published.

To : Mon

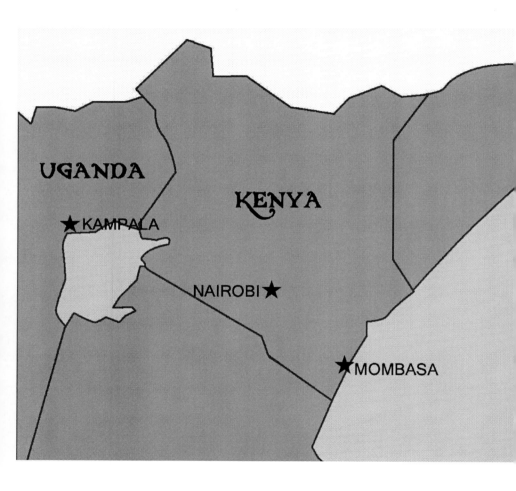

CHAPTER 1

July 1977

The game of dominoes was well under way by the time I arrived. I'm glad I missed the start. The part I did witness has haunted me ever since.

I can't be sure because I wasn't there, but the players would have been in a line when the master of ceremonies explained the rules. He was still there when I was ushered unceremoniously into the dungeon. He was a soldier and, like his assistants, he wore a green uniform and big black boots. It was impossible to tell the occupations of the dozen players just by looking at them because they were to a man naked. Naked they came into this world and naked again . . .

The rules were simple.

Domino number two would deal Domino number one a single, hopefully fatal, blow with a sledgehammer which he would then pass on to Domino number three. No. 3 would then dispatch *him* in the same way. And so along the line. I doubt if the officer had disclosed who would batter to death the last man in the row. When I arrived and became that last man I quickly picked up the rules and chose not to ask who was going to murder me.

The sledgehammer rose and fell, and a fourth enemy, real or imagined, of Idi Amin Dada, fell lifeless to the floor. The hammer followed him, dropped in despair by one who knew that he was to be the next to die.

Thud.

I have always hated dominoes.

One man refused to play his role in the game of death, whether from principle or paralysis I do not know. He stood, slack-jawed, and looked with horror at the sledgehammer. One of the soldiers, keen to impress his superior, barked a command in a Ugandan dialect I did not know. (There was not, nor *is* there, a Ugandan dialect that I *do* know.) Number seven made no move to obey the order. He was cut in half by a burst of submachine gun bullets ordered nonchalantly by the officer and loosed eagerly by his subordinate.

Thud! The game was getting perilously close to home base.

(If I am giving the impression that I, as twelfth man, was regarding this spectacle of savagery with equanimity, forget it. The initial indignity of being seen to have the least large penis in the group was not a long-lasting emotion. Fear took over: raw, gut-wrenching terror at what was about to happen.)

Thud! Three to go. Then me.

Suddenly, the door clanked open. A man stood framed on the threshold. He crouched so that he could see inside and then, ducking under the lintel, entered the cellar. He wore a faded uniform with bright green circles the size to half crowns in rows across his massive chest. I, like everybody else in the cellar, watched him in silence. He was an enormous man. He had short, black curly hair, protruding eyes and a large nose overhanging generous lips that relaxed to reveal white teeth. He was unarmed and yet he was the most dangerous occupant of the cellar. He was there, not by order, but by choice - for pleasure. He counted silently the dominoes yet to fall. He looked disappointed, perhaps that so few were still standing. He was joined a moment later by a white man wearing a tan safari suit. This man stood by, in attendance, and did not utter a word.

The guards had snapped to attention a second after the giant entered. They looked frightened at first, but they relaxed when he waved them at ease with an enormous paw and crossed to take his position in the queue between prisoners ten and eleven.

Thud!

Number nine was gone; it was the late arrival's turn to wield the hammer. He was side on to me when he snatched the weapon from the yielding fingers of his intended victim. His face was bathed in sweat and his lips were drawn back in a horrible leer. The sledgehammer rose slowly, easily, and then descended with thunderous force, decelerating abruptly as it made contact with its target. The lifeless victim fell.

The transformation on the big man's face was instantaneous. His crazed eyes calmed and a jolly smile replaced the look of insane hatred that had been exorcised by his act of violence. He glanced at the white man who had been watching. "You want a turn, Bob?" he asked. Bob shook his head, apparently content to enjoy his pleasures vicariously. The big man grinned more broadly. He said something to the soldiers and they sniggered dutifully. His eyes swivelled back to inspect the carnage on the cellar floor and then he looked at me. He didn't say anything else. He tossed the sledgehammer into the air as if it were made of balsa wood and caught it deftly by its head of steel. The wooden haft he offered to me. His mocking smile was fraught with challenge.

CHAPTER 2

May 1977

Snyder and Mercouri were already in the bar when I arrived at the Ritz. Snyder stood up, held out a welcoming hand and smiled. "Good to see you again, Doctor King," he said.

"It seems a long time, Colonel." It had only been a few weeks, but it felt like months.

"Hi, Mike," Dave Mercouri waved his welcome. "Glad you decided to come. What'll it be?"

"Whisky and water, please."

Dave nodded to the barman who turned to the row of optics behind them. "Anything but Teachers?" Dave smiled at our private joke. While we waited, I studied Jim Snyder as he studied me. Dave watched us both and there was silence at the bar - a not uncomfortable silence, one that would only be broken when the chance of interruption was nil - we had not met for an evening of small talk.

Snyder was a broad man and six feet tall. He

was a South African, in his late forties. His hair was black and curly and he had a lived-in face with a wide forehead and prominent cheekbones. His teeth were white and even and contrasted with a tan etched deeply into his skin by a tropical sun. His American companion was even bigger with thick brown hair and a ready smile. Both were dressed in dark suits, white shirts and black shoes. Standing at attention by Mercouri's feet was a black attaché case.

When my drink arrived we toasted each other and when the barman retreated Snyder said: "I feel that perhaps an apology is in order. The Seychelles affair was not our most successful operation."

You can say that again, I thought. Aloud, I said, "Not at all; it was just bad luck."

Snyder grimaced. He knew and I knew and he knew that I knew that bad luck had nothing to do with the failure of the Seychelles mission; Snyder was a professional. So was Dave Mercouri and so had I been for a short time in the Islands of Love. Snyder and his men had been hired in London to restore the recently overthrown Government of Seychelles to the control of its pre-coup masters. From a base in South Africa they had sailed to Mahe, suffering en route an injury to their medical officer. This had led them to impress my good self as temporary replacement doctor and spy.

I had done what I had been asked to do - brilliantly, I thought - but the mission had been aborted because of lack of funding: Snyder's responsibility and cross to bear. I had ended up being kicked out of Seychelles and had bumped into Mercouri in London soon after my return to the UK. A new venture was being planned and I had been invited to meet with Snyder with a view to recruitment - voluntary this time.

"Not bad luck," Snyder said quietly. He must have been reading my thoughts. "Bad management. My fault entirely - it will not happen again."

I looked at Dave and waited for him to spring to his boss' defence, but he added nothing to Snyder's confession; he sipped his whisky and waited for the conversation to change direction.

"This time, doctor, it will be different. This time the money is up front."

Mercouri grinned. "That means you'll get paid this time, Mike."

"If I decide to join up," I pointed out to him.

"If you are invited to do so," Snyder concluded grimly.

There was an embarrassed silence.

"Hey, let's go eat, huh?" Dave suggested with forced heartiness.

Snyder shrugged.   "Good idea. You hungry, doctor?"

I nodded.

"Then let's go."

I followed the two soldiers into the dining room where we were led to a corner table by the restaurant manager. During dinner I must have won Snyder over with my sparkling wit (and gentle remindings that my part in the Seychelles affair had indeed been flawlessly executed). I had really turned up at the Ritz to scrounge a good meal, but now . . . now I wanted in. Perhaps the wine seduced me, or perhaps it was the promise, made by Mercouri at the same time as the invitation to dine, of five thousand dollars up front and "five times that much on completion". Either way, I was eager to enlist and it seemed that Snyder was now as keen as Mercouri to sign me up.

No details of the forthcoming operation were mentioned during the fish course, nor, indeed, while we enjoyed the entree, but as soon as we settled into port and cheese, Snyder said softly, "We're going to Uganda. We're going to take out Idi Amin."

I nodded and automatically switched on my

poker face. I wasn't going to show surprise. I was a veteran with two weeks experience and if he had said that we were going to Moscow to take out Leonid Breshnev, I would have said, "OK da!" Tough guy - that was me.   "Not by submarine, I trust," was my only comment.

Mercouri guffawed and Snyder grinned.

I smiled modestly. I was a great kidder.

"No," Snyder agreed, "not by sea.   We're parachuting   in."

The smile left my face faster than a card sharp deals seconds and my poker face turned baize green at the gills.

Mercouri guffawed and Snyder grinned.

I stared at one and then at the other.

"You're joking!" I gasped at last. Both men shook their heads.

"No joke," Snyder said. "We're jumping in. But," he relented, "not you and Dave. You'll be going ahead by plane to Entebbe. Like you did on Mahe. You'll be the advance party."

Relief flooded through me. It wasn't that I was afraid of heights - or even of falling - it was the landing that scared me to death. And now they knew. But they didn't seem to care and so neither did I.

"Dave mentioned a down payment," I muttered.

"Seems fair," Snyder replied. "Especially after you did the last job for nothing." He nodded to Mercouri who lifted the attaché case on to his knees, twiddled the combination, opened the lid and took out a bulky white envelope. He passed it to Snyder who gave it to me.

"Consider this a belated payment for the Seychelles job. The Uganda money comes later. It might be better if you didn't count it here."

I flicked back the flap with my thumb and felt a warm glow spread throughout my body as I recognised in the thick sheaf one hundred dollar bills - lots of them. I wanted to jump up and down and cheer and buy everybody a drink, but I sat still, permitted a tiny smile to crease my lips and slipped the envelope into my inside pocket with a nonchalance I thought made up for my previous show of alarm.

Snyder stood up and offered a friendly hand.

"Dave'll fill you in on the details. I have another appointment but I'll see you tomorrow. Until then, Mike." He waved his hand and left the restaurant. It was the first time he had called me by my Christian name and I felt ridiculously pleased; the bulge over my heart made my happiness complete. The doubts and fears would come later, but at that moment I was ready to take out Idi Amin.

"When do we go in, Dave?"

"In about a month," he replied. "Just enough time to get you into some sort of shape."

"Shape!"

"Of course. You can't be a good mercenary unless you can dodge the bullets you know."

"I could try,"

He smiled. "So, tomorrow we are off to camp in the country. Where are you staying tonight, by the way?"

"I'm booked into a bed and breakfast."

"You'll manage to get back there OK?"

"I think I'll manage. I'm a big boy, you know."

"Right. Be back here tomorrow at eleven."

"OK. Where are you staying tonight by the way?"

He grinned. "With a friend. Do you want anything else, Mike?" When I shook my head he raised a hand and the waiter appeared. Dave asked for the bill and, when it came, he paid in cash.

"Right, compadre, until tomorrow. Don't get into any trouble - and watch your money. You're gonna have to work hard for the next instalment."

He left me alone in the Ritz Hotel with five thousand dollars in my pocket, a smile on my lips and a song in my heart.

CHAPTER 3

The waiter came back over to the table.

"Would m'sieu care for anything further?" he asked.

M'sieu thought for a while. A cognac to sip and time to collect his thoughts seemed a good idea. But not at the table. Let the chaps clear up; m'sieu would go to the bar.

So I told him no and, standing, I aped Napoleon, feeling for the first time since my deportation, not a right tit, but a man of means. I sauntered into the bar and ordered a gentleman's measure of Hennessy XO. I took a seat in the corner of the room and admired its lavish decor. Hidden lighting revealed a discreet pastel colour scheme: the carpet was a thick pile Axminster in pale tan and the curtains were of heavy, cream-coloured silk. The furniture itself consisted of brocade armchairs arranged around mahogany tables.

What a fine hotel, I thought.

A suitable place of repose for a well-to-do

young mercenary, I agreed.

Better than a tatty old guest house.

So check in here; it doesn't seem all that busy.

What about the guest house?

What about *the guest house?*

I've paid in advance.

Cheapskate! How much?

A fiver.

A whole fiver!

And my suitcase is there.

What's in it?

Well, socks, and a couple of shirts and -

Leave them!

Leave them?

Get some decent stuff tomorrow - you can afford it now.

That's right. So I can.

And so it was settled. I finished my brandy and asked at reception if there was room at the inn. There was: a single room with en suite facilities for a piddling hundred quid a night.

"Do you wish your baggage taken up now, sir?"

"Er . . . no - I'll get it later. Thanks."

The receptionist, a tall lady with big tits but on the old side - she must have been forty - snapped her fingers and a sixteen year old bell hop materialised to lead me to room 625. I tipped him with a 50p coin upon which he looked with contempt.

It was eleven o'clock. I had twelve hours before I was to meet Mercouri and be taken to the camp and I was determined to make the most of these last hours of freedom. What I needed was action. I picked up the phone and made my request to the front desk. Half an hour later, a fiver lighter, but with $5,000 in my inside pocket, I was shown into the main hall of the Cardinal Gaming Club.

It was busy. All eight roulette wheels were full and the blackjack counters were doing a roaring trade. From time to time a beaming or an ashen or a poker-faced punter would vacate a chair and be swallowed up in the throng; his place would be filled before the next cut of the cards or the next spin of the wheel. The air was blue with smoke, the babble incomprehensible. Dinner jackets rubbed shoulders with more casual gear, summer frocks with evening gowns. The croupiers, smart in their black tuxedos and white frilly shirts, raked and dealt and spun the wheels without expression. The controllers sat on high-backed chairs, their eyes never still.

"Mesdames et messieurs, faites vos jeux."

"Rien ne va plus."

"Zero!"

"Merde!" A little bald man who looked like Peter Ustinov playing Hercule Poirot muttered his disappointment while the croupiers worked overtime to clear the baize of its chips and plaques.

I wandered to the next table and positioned myself directly behind the most glamorous, unattached woman I could see. I willed her to win. If she did, she would know it was because I had brought her luck. She would smile her thanks as she cashed in her chips and I would bow and suggest a cognac.

"Thank you, kind sir, I would be delighted," she would reply. We would have a couple of nightcaps and then, before you could say "Napoleon Brandy" we would be back in her hotel room and I would be unclipping her bra. And then I would . . .

My reverie was shattered when the lady in question turned her coiffured head and rasped in a hoarse whisper, "Fuck off, fatso! Is your name Jonah or something? I haven't won as much as an even money bet since you arrived!"

I stepped back as if slapped. I looked pityingly at the painted whore and thought, "American bitch!" I back-pedalled to the next table. As I watched the action there I fingered lovingly my own plaques. There were ten of them, each worth fifty quid and they were safely in my trousers pockets.

You won't win anything while they're there, scaredy, I told myself.

Won't lose too much either, I retorted silently.

True, but did you come here to play roulette or just to play with yourself?

All right! All right!

I hate being hassled.

I withdrew one hand from a pocket. It contained five plaques that were the size of a credit card. I placed them on red. All of them. There was a sudden silence. Then the table inspector spoke. "I am sorry, m'sieur, but the maximum stake for an even money bet at this table is two hundred pounds. Table number one is the table for you."

I was aware of being watched by a dozen pairs of eyes. I flushed and leaned forward to retrieve my chips. Then, as I looked up, I realised that the expressions on the faces around me were full of admiration rather than envy (except that of Hercule Poirot - the poisonous little frog just stared at me spitefully). I smiled and murmured, "So sorry. Table number one you say?"

"Oui, m'sieur. There." He pointed to the top of the room where a roulette table stood on a dais and was cordoned off by a wine-coloured rope of velvet. I headed for it and reached it as 33 black came up. When invited to play I leaned carelessly over a seated blonde woman in blue and placed my bet: two hundred and fifty pounds on red. The woman, about to complain at my rudeness, changed her mind when she saw the size of my wager and bestowed on me instead a haughty smile. I returned it with interest and then moved round to the other side of the table to get a better look at her. As I walked I suddenly realised the enormity of my risk. I wasn't a gambler - not really - maybe a tenner on a sure thing, but not ever in this league. When I had bought my chips the only reason I hadn't taken a fiver's worth of 25p tokens was because I was being watched by a wizened old goat wearing a monocle and a startling blonde who was dripping diamonds; I had been too embarrassed not to buy high denomination plaques. Two hundred and fifty quid! I can't risk that, I thundered to myself. I thought to cancel my bet but there wasn't time to get back round the table - the croupier had started to spin the wheel.

Then it came to me. *Bet the same amount on black!*

What if zero comes up?

It's 36 to 1 it doesn't.

Are you sure?

Christ!

Right.

The croupier called 'Rien ne va plus'. I stretched forward to place my second bet and, at the same time, glanced around the table. Beautiful, if baleful eyes stared into my own - eyes that had watched me back red a few seconds before. I hesitated.

Oh, so what?

I dropped the plaques on black.

"Mes apologies, m'sieur," the croupier said, "mais vous etes trop tard."

I was too late! I looked at the man blankly as

he raked my counters back to my still outstretched hand.

The white ivory ball came off the bend at the top of the wheel and click-clacked its way over the frets around its perimeter. I watched, appalled. I had gambled, albeit unwillingly, two hundred and fifty pounds! The chattering stopped. I was sweating and my eyes watered as I strove to fight off the dizzy turn that threatened to fell me. I heard the words: "Trente-deux; rouge; pair; passe", but their significance escaped me. I blinked. I blinked again. My vision cleared. Red! It was in the red! I had won! I had won two hundred and fifty pounds!

My hands trembled as I bent forward, scooped up my pile of plaques and stuffed them into my pockets. God! I had to have a drink. Lurching in a way that denied such a need I made my way to the bar that adjoined the gaming hall.

"Brandy! Large!"

I took the drink to an empty table and drank half of it in a gulp. The trembling subsided. That was so easy, I thought. Two hundred and fifty quid. Tax free. Easier even than the five grand from Snyder. Why not have a real go, I thought. Use only their money. Why not? Why not indeed? I finished my drink and bounded back to the table.
Mike King M.D., Soldier of Fortune, Entrepreneur

was going to take 'em on!

I slammed £200 on black.

It won.

I let it ride.

It won again.

One more time.

Black.

And again.

"I am verr sorry, M'sieu, but ze limit for even money bets is £1,500."

"All right. The limit - but on red!"

With an expert flick of his spatula the croupier divided the plaques into two unequal piles and lifted the larger one on to the red compartment. The smaller one he stacked at the table's edge in front of me.

Red!

Thank God I had changed my bet!

Red!

And again!

Black!

Red!

Fourteen times in a row I successfully bet the limit. The casino was in an uproar. The table was surrounded six deep by an enthralled audience, some of whom were betting my colours.

The limit - red!

Black!

The spell was broken. I stared at the baize as £1,500 were shovelled to the far end of the table. I shook my head and refocused on the mountain of silver plaques in front of me.

"You have over twenty thousand pounds there, my friend. Congratulations."

I jerked my head to the left and looked into the eyes of the lady in blue. I smiled a slow smile.

"Thank you, madame, you have brought me luck. Perhaps a celebratory Cognac?"

"Thank you, kind sir, I would be delighted."

I followed her to the caisse where I cashed in my chips.

"M'sieu would like a cheque?"

"M'sieu would like cash!"

He arched his eyebrows.

"Would M'sieu accept £5,000 in cash and a cheque for the balance - a cashier's cheque of course?"

I thought it over. Maybe it had been a bad night. Maybe they were short of cash. Maybe I would be safer with a cheque and so I said OK, a cheque would be good for the balance.

"Not going to count it, . . er . . ?"

"Mike. No, no need . . er . . ?"

"Natasha. Where then?"

"Where?"

"Your place or mine. I have a bottle of Remy Martin and I am only minutes from here."

"Your place sounds fine."

I pocketed my loot and we headed for her place.

****

Natasha had many wonderful qualities. First

of all she was awfully easy to look at. She had long blonde hair, chemically assisted, but soft and sparkling. She reminded me facially of a fair Claudia Cardinale and bodily of a dark Marilyn Monroe (but more of that later).

Secondly, her cognac was excellent. She had taken my arm as we left the casino and murmured, "Taxi". We hopped into the first of a line of cabs and she directed the driver to the Hotel Belvedere. The cabby, a middle-aged man with a handlebar moustache arched an eyebrow, shrugged and then drove us a hundred yards before stopping outside a structure of glass that bore the neon legend, "Hotel Belvedere". I arched *my* eyebrow, shrugged and gave him a fiver.

Natasha's pad was a suite of rooms on the seventh floor overlooking the Houses of Parliament. It was nearly as nice as my own room at the Ritz. The living room was furnished with a glass-topped table, two easy chairs and a bar in one corner that was attended by a pair of high stools. She took up position behind the counter and I climbed on to one of the stools.

"Is Cognac OK or would you like something else?" she asked.

"Cognac's fine," I said.

She poured two healthy measures into crystal balloon glasses and cupped her hands around the one she kept for herself. Every finger that I could see sparkled with a stone that looked the real McCoy to me. Here was a lady with more money than I had! For several moments we did not speak. She was allowing me time, I suppose, to relive my coup at the tables and perhaps to anticipate exploring in the near future her bedroom (and her). And so I should have been. And so I was, but not exclusively. A plan was forming in my mind that I liked and wanted to develop. I now had as much money as I was to realise from the African trip. So who needed it? Mosquitoes and prickly heat? A six inch nail driven into the forehead by a baboon in uniform with wooden splinters under his fingernails? Not me!

"A penny for them," she murmured.

"I was thinking about a trip to South America," I lied.

"Business?"

"Pleasure." I placed my hand on top of hers and stroked the rockstrewn valley at the top of her third and fourth fingers. She smiled 'yes'. "Better get in practice then," she whispered.

Still holding my hand she glided from behind

the bar and perched herself upon my lap. She entwined her arms around my neck and brushed the hair at the base of my neck with a carefully careless finger. I tickled the insides of her ears and she purred. We kissed. Her tongue darted in and out of my mouth. I found the zip at the back of her dress and slowly pulled it down. I fondled the bottom of her spine and then I fondled her bottom. She squirmed. She stood up and, with a wriggle, freed herself from her dress. It slid to the floor and draped itself across the pile carpet. She took a step back, unclipped her bra and finally stepped out of her pants; her stockings she kept on. I struggled out of my own clothes and we did it once on the bar counter. The next time was on her bed. When she said, "Let's have one for the road", I thought she meant let's have another fuck and I groaned (I wasn't as young as I used to be). But she only meant another drink (and I'll never be too old to refuse that).

"I'll get it," she said. "Cognac?"

"Fine."

When she came back we leaned against the headboard, half in, half out of the bed.

"Here's to South America," she whispered.

"Have you ever been there?"

She nodded. "I spent a summer in Buenos Aires. I can recommend it. It has everything."

"Tell me about . . . everything."

She started to tell me about the Teatro Nacional Cervantes and a district called La Buca where there are dozens of Italian Cantinas. Somewhere, however, between "Italian" and "Cantinas" I began to feel drowsy. I was aware of her taking the glass from my hand. I felt very sleepy. I nestled my head on her shoulder as she described some of the most outrageous nightclubs in the world. Then I must have fallen asleep.

****

Natasha's less admirable qualities were: she was a thief and she used drugs - on other people! When I awoke I found that not only was I alone but also that my wallet was empty. She had lifted my winnings and also the money I had got from Snyder. I now had less then a tenner to my name.

Boiling with anger and frustration, I got dressed and dashed down to reception to be told that Mrs Smith had checked out only a couple of hours ago. Mrs Smith! That was all I needed! Why could she not have been the Countess of Paris or something and easy to trace? Not that that would have made much difference - I'm a doctor, not a debt collector!

You are also a soldier, King! A mercenary! A member of a band!

I stood in the foyer of the Hotel Belvedere and fumed. Twenty thousand poundsand five grand! My independence! Evaporated as had that . . . that bitch! And she'd presumably paid her bill with *my* money! Which reminded me: I owed the Ritz a hundred quid. I couldn't ask Mercouri for a loan. He'd want to know what had happened to my bundle and even if I didn't tell him about my win at the casino, he would still have fun if I told him anything like the truth.

"What? Five thousand dollars for a broad? Oh, but you laid her twice! Well, that's not so bad! Only two and a half grand a fuck!"

Two and a half grand nothing! They were the most expensive screws I have ever heard about! Twelve thousand quid apiece! I wanted to curl up and die.

I felt no guilt whatsoever about not squaring that account at the Ritz. I went back of course, but I intercepted Mercouri before he could enter the revolving door. Then we went off to camp.

CHAPTER 4

I never did find out where the camp was situated. When we had settled ourselves into his nondescript Ford estate, Dave had produced a piece of velvet which he handed to me. It was black, like my mood. Deja vu, I thought. I remembered the morning, only a few weeks back aboard an inflatable dinghy in the middle of the Indian Ocean, when a similar blindfold had been offered to me by a gorilla who turned out to be one of the band. On that occasion, an automatic pistol levelled at my stomach persuaded me to put it on. But why this time? I felt hurt and annoyed. Dave read the displeasure in my eyes before I could express it in words and held up his hands in appeasement.

"Orders, doc. We're all operating on a need-to-know basis. Only Snyder and I know where the camp is - the other men arrived blindfold as well."

Mollified, but still muttering about lack of loyalty and trust, I checked my watch and slipped the blindfold over my eyes; I would concentrate on gauging our speed so that I would be able to work out the distance, if not the direction, we were to travel from the capital. My cunning plan didn't work of course.

Dave tried to make small talk, but I was in a sulk. I was thinking about twenty thousand pounds. Not to mention five grand. He gave up and, instead of talking, whistled tunelessly for the next hour and a half. I dozed. Hundred pound notes floated from a high bar counter and disappeared into the bosom of a woman in blue.

And then I was in a restaurant - very expensive, very chic. The linen was white like the Wedgewood service; the cutlery was solid silver. Topless waitresses floated from table to table as if they were on castors. Other diners looked round from time to time at me and my companion. The jealousy and hatred in their expressions surprised me at first, but I ignored them and concentrated instead on what my dinner partner was saying to me.

A waitress with particularly shapely breasts and walnut nipples appeared at my shoulder. In her hand she held a silver tray and on the tray was a note. It was addressed to me and was signed, "Snyder". I read it and, with a smile, passed it to the enormous black man in the uniform of a general who shared my chateaubriand. I stood up and, knowing that Snyder was watching, announced clearly: "Why, Jim, I'm only taking out Idi Amin."

As one, the other diners turned and hurled at me and my guest, invective and sole meuniere and boeuf bourguignon and plates and knives. I twisted my body to escape being hit and, in so doing, jostled Dave's arm and myself awake.

"Hey, what the - ?"

"Oh, sorry, Dave, just temporarily lost my balance."

"You're a dangerous man to drive with," he muttered.

"Do we have far to go?" I asked.

"Not too far."

I clenched my teeth and then remembered my dream.

"I just dreamed that I was taking Idi Amin out - to dinner!"

He chuckled but made no comment.

We drove on in silence for another half hour during which time I came to a decision. I would brood no longer about my lost money, but when I returned from Uganda I would use some of my wages to find that bitch in blue!

Then we stopped. Dave switched off the

engine and announced, "We've arrived."

I raised a tentative hand to the blindfold. "Is it OK to . . . ?"

"Go ahead."

I slipped the velvet over my head and flicked it on to the shelf above the dashboard. Everything was dark. I did not know yet whether the car was parked in or out of doors. I looked in the direction of my watch and pressed the tiny button that activated its light source.

Blur past blur.

I heard Dave heave himself out of the car, but I decided to stay put until my normal twenty-twenty vision was restored.

Ten past blur.

The driver's door reopened and Dave's fuzzy silhouette appeared.

"Are you going to stay in there all day?" he demanded.

"I'm coming. I'm coming. I still can't see, you know."

"Oh."

Twelve minutes past two. (We had been driving for nearly three hours - a hundred and fifty, two hundred miles, or merely ever-decreasing circles?)

"Yes I can! Here I come!"

I opened my door and joined him outside.

Inside. We were in a garage.

Suddenly someone threw a switch and I found myself sightless again - blinded this time by a dazzling sixty-watter above. I closed my eyes and counted stars. Dave laughed. He took hold of my arm and led me over a concrete floor and into another room through doors that I heard him close behind us. I wondered if I was going into this new operation with my eyes open. The new room moved. Up the way. I opened my eyes again and a set of lift buttons came into focus.

"This is camp?" I asked.

"This is camp."

****

I hated camp. There was no booze and no women; just backache and heartbreak and the company of a crowd of gorillas who wanted to play soldiers. I was there twenty nine days. And nights.

I got to know Dave Mercouri pretty well and, to a lesser extent, Snyder. I renewed my acquaintance with Jean Marc with whom I had shared a cabin in Seychelles and I met the other men and got on fine with them.

And, on the first morning after I'd been kitted out by the quartermaster, I met Beresford and Heck in the refectory.

Refectory. A misnomer. Mess hall? Ridiculous. Even Ward Room did no justice to the chamber that Dave and I entered on the ground floor of this country seat that was camp. It was about fifty feet square and thirty feet high. The walls were panelled in a dark wood that looked rich and warm. They were bespattered with minor masterpieces. A large mahogany table occupied the space in front of a huge bay window that overlooked a croquet lawn and a long sideboard stood in front of a hatch in the right hand wall. On it was an assortment of cereals, juices, cold meats, cheeses and fruit. Scattered across the parquet floor were half a dozen smaller tables. If the entire band ate together, I thought, there could not be more than forty all told. Forty men against the Ugandan army!

At the top table Jim Snyder sat alone drinking coffee. "Morning, Dave, doctor," he said cheerfully.

"Morning . . . er . . "

"Jim."

"Morning, Jim."

"Sleep well?"

"Yes thanks. You?"

He nodded and waved airily towards the sideboard. "Help yourself - and shout through the hatch to Heck if you want a cooked breakfast."

"Egg and bacon?" Dave enquired. "Porridge?"

I shook my head. "Coffee and toast."

"Me too. Sit down. Today, I'll be waiter."

I sat down beside Jim Snyder.

"You look very smart, Doctor. The uniform becomes you."

I grinned self-consciously and patted my tunic flat across my stomach. Dave planked a pot of steaming coffee and a rack of toast on the table and sat opposite me. "Mike was disappointed to miss the run this morning," he said. Snyder saw my sickly grin and clucked sympathetically.

"Don't worry, Mike. Your time will come,"

I decided to clutch the nettle.

"Dave has told me we'll be here about a month. What exactly am I expected to do in that time - besides taking sick call, of course?"

The two officers exchanged glances and smiled.

"I've told you before, Mike," Dave explained. "This is not the regular army. You will not be overwhelmed by ailing men complaining of stomach aches or sore feet or migraines. These men are professionals. They don't get sick and, even if they do, they don't go running to the nearest pill-pusher."

"So what am I here for?" I demanded. Pill-pusher indeed!

Snyder took up the briefing.

"Even these guys need treatment if they stop a bullet, doctor. Your medical services could - will - be required in Africa. For the next few weeks I want you to get to know the men and to get fit. Don't worry - it'll be in stages. We don't want you on any sick list. And," he concluded, "you have to rehearse your mission with Dave before the rest of us go in."

I drank my coffee to hide my dismay. So this was it. The deep end. And I had less than a month to figure out a way of escape. Get fit; get to know the chaps; get word perfect for the last act. One step at a time, King!

"How many men are there to get to know?" I asked.

"There are thirty men, three officers - and yourself," Dave replied. "You know Jim and me; you've met Jean-Marc. Only thirty to go."

"It's not the biggest army in the world," I observed.

Snyder put down his empty cup and stood up. He had obviously more important things to do. "Doctor," he said, "it is not our intention to take on the entire Ugandan army. Our assignment is to locate and neutralise its commanding officer, General Amin.   And now I must get on. Dave, I'll see you in my office in an hour after you've introduced Mike to the men." He nodded once more to each of us and then marched out of the room.

Dave poured more coffee.

Just then the door opened and in they trooped: the dirty couple of dozen; the cross-country runners; my fellow mercenaries and classmates.

"Wa-tu wale wa-mefika," said Dave.

"Huh?" said I.

"That was Swahili. It means, 'those people have arrived' - 'here they come!'"

"Oh, right. I'll remember that."

We watched 'those people' serve themselves from the sideboard and call orders for hot breakfasts through the hatch. They all seemed to speak English, but if they were all English, then, verily, it had to be unto the second generation - at least! There were white men, black men, yellow men and even a red man. There were big men and small men, thin men and fat men. That such diversification could exist in a sample of just a few dozen was extraordinary.

One soldier disengaged himself from the others and, carrying a plateful of bacon, sausages and eggs, sat in the chair vacated by Snyder.

"Morning, Dave." he said.

"Hi, Chris. Meet Mike King. Mike, this is Captain Chris Beresford, officer in charge of training in our little outfit. Chris is from Cardiff"

Beresford was a man of about my own height and looked about thirty. He was handsome in a boyish way and had wavy fair hair parted on the right, blue eyes and a weak chin. To this day I do not know why, but he took an instant dislike to me and so, of course, I promptly returned his animosity with interest. It is possible that when we shook hands distaste showed in my expression - distaste at the clammyness of his limp grasp. Or perhaps it was his greeting that provoked a reaction in me which, in turn, caused him to develop his antipathy towards me.

"Ah, the English amateur," he said.

"Captain Berrysdown," I returned icily.

"Beresford, actually, old chap." He looked at Mercouri. "Is the new doctor deaf, Dave?"

I hate being ignored - especially by thick Welsh gits and more especially by thick Welsh gits who are to be in charge of the training of my body. I kept my expression frostily neutral as Dave changed the subject.

"How are the boys shaping up, Chris?"

Beresford gave me a last look of disdain down his long poncy nose and assured Mercouri that training was going well and that the boys were getting fitter by the hour. Dave nodded and then, banging his spoon on the table, called the assembly to order.

"Gentlemen. Please carry on eating. However, I would appreciate it if you would also lend an ear to what I have to say." Dave spoke slowly and clearly for the benefit, I presumed, of those for whom English was not the mother tongue. "I would like to introduce to you our new medical officer, Doctor Mike King from the North of England."

I was not sure of the form but I grinned self-consciously and half rose from my seat at the table.

"Doctor King has some experience of serving as a soldier of fortune. In fact, this is his second week."

A few of the men laughed, but the others continued to stare at either me or Dave Mercouri. The latter went on to explain:

"He joined us briefly on our last mission in the Seychelles. Some of you might remember seeing him on the good ship Guinivere."

Jean-Marc bobbed his head and grinned at me from a table where he ate breakfast with three other men. One was black and looked like an elder and tougher brother to Sydney Poitier. The second man had to turn round to see us. He was white, slight and nondescript; he would have made a good undercover man. The last soldier at the table was a big fellow with red hair.

Dave sat down again and the men resumed eating. Conversations sprang up at all the tables, but the talk was circumspect, muted, even. The chat at our table was laboured. Beresford communicated with Mercouri, but he made it clear that my presence inhibited any meaningful discussion. I spoke to Dave and studiously ignored Beresford. Mercouri, caught in the middle, clearly cared neither for the situation nor for the atmosphere, but he could not see how to influence it quickly and for the better. He decided to leave us to it and excused himself, saying that he had to meet with the colonel.

After a minute and a half of silence, I pushed my chair back and left Beresford to finish his breakfast alone. I had intended following Mercouri from the room but two things changed my mind. First, I recalled Snyder's request that I get to know the men and secondly, I saw that this was an ideal opportunity to annoy Beresford. I lifted an empty chair from a neighbouring table and invited myself to join Jean-Marc's quartet.

The four men rose in unison and I was introduced to Joel Lo Pinto from Mozambique, Burt McMichael from the United States and Liam McGurk from County Limerick. We all sat and I was offered coffee. Jean-Marc provided the extra cup when I said yes.

"The doctor and me," Jean-Marc declared, "we were roommates in the sub, eh, mon brave? The doctor is a very early riser," he added with a grin. I nodded non-committally. This was neither the time nor the place to explain that my lark-like evacuation of our shared cabin had been prompted by Jean-Marc's incredibly loud snoring.

"I'll never forget that night, Jean-Marc," I said and looked round the table. "Have you been together long?"

McGurk elected himself spokesman.

"Jean-Marc and I have four years together. Joel joined up - was it three years ago, Joel?" The black man nodded. "And Burt signed up for the Seychelles trip - he likes tropical cruises, is that not so, Burt?"

We chatted for some minutes - long enough for Captain Beresford to tire of his own company and to brush past our table and march (or was it stalk?) from the room. McGurk's eyes followed him and danced mischievously; Jean-Marc's look was one of contempt. I would have loved to pay a penny for their thoughts but, of course, to ask was out of the question. Beresford and I were officers while the four men at whose table I sat were not. I knew the code; I had seen it in the movies often enough.

"Prick!"

My eyebrows shot up. What about the code? I thundered silently. It was Burt McMichael who had uttered the word, quietly, without venom, but with

46

irrefutable certainty. I coughed to hide my embarrassment - and glee - and surveyed the others over a protective hand. Nods of agreement greeted the condemnation. I resisted the urge to ask for an explanation (I did not want to get a reputation for encouraging disloyal talk, did I?) but I hoped for clarification of that monosyllabic description. I was not disappointed.

"Bigot!" Burt murmured and again his companions made no effort to defend their training officer. This was getting better and better.

"Hates blacks and Irishmen," Liam explained.

"And Americans," Burt added.

And Englishmen, I wanted to say, but just in time I remembered the code. So too, perhaps, did Jean-Marc.

"Ah, mes amis, he is not here to be liked, hein?"

"Sure, he doesn't like Belgians either," Liam pointed out.

Smiles appeared on African, American, Engish and Belgian faces to match that already plastered over the one from County Limerick.

Suddenly a bell rang. The men leapt to their

feet and dashed out as Beresford's voice, amplified and sounding metallic through a loud hailer, filled the room.

I sat in splendid isolation for about thirty seconds. Then I was blitzed by a tornado that came through a half door in the wall below the hatch. It was five feet six high, bald and frantic.

"Whit the fuck are you daein' here?" it yelled. I stared at it and thought, oh no, not that, not now: not an undersized, under-vocabularised Glaswegian!

"Are ye deif? Did ye no' hear the fuckin' bell?"

He made for my table at high speed and I flinched, sure that an attack was to be made on my person. Instead of grabbing me, however, he gathered two handfuls of plates and almost flung them through the hatch. Before he had turned to collect what remained on the table he bellowed, "Huv ye loast yer fuckin' tongue an' a'?"

"I . . . er . . . "

"Aye, aye, right enough," he interrupted. "Is that a' ye kin fuckin' say?"

"I'm new here," I managed to explain. I was careful to roll my 'r's so that he might recognise in me an honorary Scot and kindred spirit.

"Frae Newcastle, eh?"

"Aye, that I am."

He sniffed. "Christ! Another fuckin' Sassanach!"

It sounded like - it *was* - an accusation.

"Ah've goat an awfy pain in ma arse. Dye want tae take a look at it?"

I hesitated, thinking, you *are* a pain in the arse.

"I thought ye widnae!" he laughed. "Ah'm glad yer no' a fuckin' poof tho'. Ah wis jest testin' ye. Ah've jest goat piles," he said as an afterthought.

I looked at the little man with distaste and was about to give him a mouthful when I remembered something Dave Mercouri had said at the Sunset Hotel on Mahe. When I had pointed out the chef to him there he had bounded across the room and, to the amazement of the Seychellois, had shaken his hand hugely and introduced himself. On his return to our table, he had whispered an explanation for his quixotic behaviour. "Ya gotta give the cook a big hello - in case he poisons ya!"

The little nyaff with the shit on his tongue and

piles up his arse was the cook. Quick, King, the olive branch,

"I've got an excellent cream for piles," I offered.

"Och, ah dinnae want anything *fer* piles - ah need something tae get rid o' the fuckers!"

The cook was a comedian! I forced my lips into a grin that I felt would have sat well on the jaws of a hyena. "It's good stuff," I insisted. "I'll drop some in to you. You can always give it a try."

"Ay, a' right. But now, get the fuck out o' here. Ah've goat tae get this shite-house cleaned up fer dinner time."

He attacked the next table and, gratefully, I made my escape.

One day at the camp was just like all the rest. We ran and we wrestled - even the medic! - and we learnt karate and I gave lessons in first aid for God's sake! It was truly a terrible time and whenever I remember it I try to forget it. I was glad when the training was over and the mission was about to begin. But if I had known what was in store for me I would not have been so eager to quit the peaceful English countryside.

CHAPTER 5

The plan was simple.   Snyder, Beresford and
the rest of the men would drive to London in a
removal van and then fly out to Durban.   There they
would await our signal from Kampala. We -
Mercouri and I - were to take the Ford to Heathrow,
fly direct to Uganda and make contact with a certain
Joseph Mawembe at Makerere University.

"Why me?" I had asked.

"You're a doctor. So is Mawembe. You go
as you; Dave travels as David Stavros, your
assistant. Unless, of course, you'd rather do some
parachute training?"

"No, no, I only wondered!"

Mawembe, it seemed, had friends close to
Amin - contacts who had not, as yet, been fed to the
crocodiles of the River Nile. He also had contacts in
South Africa - friends also of Snyder - and it was
these people who were our paymasters. We were to
meet with Mawembe and be advised by him
concerning the drop area for the rest of the gang.
They would then be contacted, parachute in and kill

Amin. Just like that.

The flight to Entebbe was uneventful. We made brief stops at Addis Ababa and Khartoum, but at neither capital were we permitted to disembark. As the aircraft came in low at our final destination I could see a green and fertile land and a lake - Victoria, the largest inland stretch of water in the world. I fancied I glimpsed the shapes of wild animals in their natural habitat, but, really, the only dangerous animal in sight was Dave Mercouri. I found out later that, in fact, there were very few wild animals left in Uganda - other than the two-legged ones: the game had been used as food by a starving population over the last years of want.

As I walked down the aluminium ladder on to the tarmac I felt the stirring of warm air that floated across the Ugandan plateau. The sun shone high and cast stunted shadows on to the tarmac. It was hot, but the heat was a dry one - quite different from the cloying atmosphere of the Seychelles where sweat could not evaporate into the already saturated air.

"I hope your papers pass muster," I muttered to my assistant. He made no reply. I wondered if he was as worried as I would have been in his shoes. Passing through immigration control and customs, however, was easier than saying, "Welcome, foreign currency". Ironically enough, most of our fellow passengers were flying on to the Seychelles. A handful of black, be-suited Africans were our only companions on our walk into the terminal building.

We looked in vain for a man in a cream safari suit wearing a red flower in his buttonhole and carrying a black attaché case in his left hand. "Let's wait in there," I suggested and made for a large sign that pointed to "Bar, Restaurant".

We sat at a table overlooking the runway and ordered two Bell beers from a bored looking waiter who seemed upset at having been disturbed. No tip for you, my man, I thought.

"We'll give him half an hour," Dave said, "and if he hasn't shown we'll take a taxi into Kampala."

I nodded. We had reservations in the Kampala International Hotel. We finished the lager undisturbed and then it was taxi time. We picked up our suitcases and, muttering dire threats against people who fail to keep appointments, walked out of the terminal building. Two ancient Peugeots occupied the taxi ranks. We bundled into the first one and directed the driver to the International Hotel.

Entebbe used to be the administrative centre in Uganda and lies twenty-two miles from the current capital city, Kampala. The connecting road, which was in a dreadful state of disrepair, was flanked by a greenery divided into shambas, or small farms. On our drive inland we saw very little life in the shambas. What we did see every few hundred yards was the military: soldiers by the lorry-load, some Entebbe-bound, others waiting in or around their transporters by the side of the road. It must have been hot work hanging about in the sun and the men we saw were sweating buckets.

We arrived in Kampala at about 4 o'clock in the afternoon and were dropped outside the monolithic International Hotel. The foyer was huge, empty of people, but it contained a dozen comfortable chairs huddled around glass-topped tables. Some of the walls supported show cases, all but one, empty. It contained a flea-bitten zebra skin stretched taut by pins that crucified it. I had no doubt that the other, vacant cases had once been filled with the skins of lion and leopard, gazelle and impala. Where were they now?   Adorning, no doubt, the apartments of the successors of ravage, the inheritors of power, the friends of the strong. Or perhaps the management had decided to remove them so that they would be safe from pillage. I didn't ask.

Reception was at the far end of the hall, opposite the plate glass doors which, I marvelled, were still intact. Between it and a backing honeycomb of numbered pigeon-holes stood a man and a woman. He was small and dapper and wore a charcoal grey suit over a white shirt. His skin was chocolatey-brown, his teeth white. His companion, who was fully six inches taller than he, was dressed in a long, floral-patterned dress. With the carriage of an empress she glided to the centre of the desk and smiled her welcome.

"Dr King and Mr Stavros," Dave announced. "We have reservations for two single rooms."

"Ah yes. We are expecting you, gentlemen."

Her voice was deep and gentle. She turned, selected a pair of keys from the gantry and said, "Please may I have your passports and would you please sign the register?"

When we obliged she pushed the keys towards us and pointed to the lift. We were to be on the fourteenth floor.

"When do we get our passports back?" Dave asked.

"Tomorrow. It is a formality."

The small man relieved her of our documents and disappeared through a door behind the desk.

There was no-one to help us with our bags so we thanked the lady and bell-hopped ourselves up to the fourteenth floor. From the numbered buttons in the lift we saw that there were fourteen floors in all, but no thirteenth; we were really on the thirteenth, but it was called the fourteenth. This made us feel very secure. Surely nothing bad could befall us on the fourteenth floor! Above us, on the fifteenth floor, was the nightclub, but we did not know this yet.

I dumped my suitcase on the bed, slid back the glass door that covered one wall and stepped out on to the narrow balcony that connected Dave's apartment with mine. He was already there, looking out over the city.

"It looks so quiet," he said.

I nodded. How long would it stay that way, I wondered?

They say that Kampala, like Rome, is a city built on seven hills, but, from our unique vantage point, we were able to count nearer seventeen. On the western horizon a range of mountains merged with the sky: the Ruwenzuris, Ptolemey's "Mountains of the Moon", which climb to seventeen thousand feet and are permanently covered by snow. Snow on the equator; I know a lot of people in Newcastle who would suggest that you should go for the cure if you were to say that in public.

Like the road from Entebbe the city was quiet

- traffic was light and mainly military. Small huddles of private cars - most looking the worse for wear - stood outside the larger buildings which we guessed were government ministries.

"What do we do now, Dave?" I asked.

"We wait."

"And if nobody comes to call?"

"If we're not contacted by tomorrow morning, we'll have to try and get in touch with Mawembe."

I nodded.

"But," Dave added, "not directly."

"Why not?"

"Because," Dave replied patiently, "if Mawembe is in trouble, we don't want to attract unwelcome attention by association."

"So . . ?"

"So, if we have heard nothing by tomorrow, you will take a taxi to Makerere University and find out if Mawembe is merely unreliable or - "

"Or," I cut in "if he is now food for the fishes - and crocodiles - in the River Nile!"

"Precisely."

I bit my lip to stop myself from asking the next, the obvious question. Dave grinned - he had thought of it also. "It's got to be you, Mike," he said reasonably. "There's no point risking both of us, and, besides, I'm just the assistant. *You're* the doctor."

How convenient, I wanted to say but, instead, I merely nodded and began to hope that our contact would materialise before breakfast.

"Right," Dave concluded, "let's get cleaned up and then we can have a stroll before dinner. Might even buy you a beer if you play your cards right."

Now that was a *good* suggestion.

My bedroom was pleasantly furnished with twin beds, ensuite bathroom and a framed picture of an elephant. The beds could easily be joined together if I got lucky. I ignored the elephant and, standing in the bath and singing "Oh, Sir Jasper", treated myself to a long, tepid shower.

Our first afternoon in Africa proved to be anticlimactic. Dave did indeed buy me a beer and I bought him one back, but we decided - he decided - that we should remain in the hotel in case someone tried to contact us. Someone did not. We dined in the large restaurant on the first floor and had for company a pair of waitresses, a trio of soberly dressed businessmen and a small group of army officers who acted as if they owned the place. They probably did. I sampled the fried tilapia, freshly caught, that day, the menu said, in Lake Victoria. Dave plumped for prawns freshly netted two months ago in some colder stretch of water. We both ate steaks, recently unfrozen and hopefully imported.

Our first night in Uganda, however, was action-packed. We sat around after dinner swapping stories and drinking short drinks slowly. At about eleven o'clock Dave suggested calling it a night and I agreed for, although I was now pretty fit, I had not, as yet, rebuilt my tolerance to alcohol and I felt tired. We said goodnight in the corridor and were swallowed up into our respective bedrooms. As I closed my door and reached for the light switch a feeling of dread engulfed me a fraction of a second before a hand cut off my air supply and another poked something hard into the small of my back.

CHAPTER 6

Fear sprang up in my gut and spread to my craw. This is it, King, I thought: the end of the line. I wondered if my antagonist would shoot me, throttle me or merely allow his body odour to suffocate me to death. He did none of these things. He whispered in my ear. "You are Doctor King?"

"Mmh!" I replied.

The clever chap seemed to understand my affirmation because he unwrapped his fingers from my lower face, switched on the light, relieved the pressure on my spine and growled, "Do not turn around."

I remained motionless.

"Can you prove that you are Doctor King?"

"Yes," I squawked in a fear-induced falsetto. "My passport . . ." was with the hotel management . . . "is with the hotel management, but I have my driving licence."

"Then produce it very carefully."

With the dexterity of a lepidopterist, I extracted my wallet from my hip pocket and, with two fingers, withdrew the required document. I passed it behind me like a relay runner offering the baton. There was a pause. Then my visitor appeared in front of me with his hand outstretched.   "I am pleased to meet you, doctor," he declared. "I am Joseph Okura, brother-in-law to Dr Mawembe. I am so sorry if I have frightened you, but in these unhappy days it is most necessary to be truly careful."

"We missed you at the airport," I remarked.

"Yes. Very sorry for that but it could not be help . . . "

His voice trailed away as he caught sight of a movement through the balcony window. I followed his gaze. The balcony was in darkness and so the silhouette that had appeared there seemed to be hovering fourteen - thirteen - stories above the ground. It was, of course, Mercouri.

"Put the gun away," I told my visitor. "It is a friend." I unlocked the sliding door and opened it. Dave walked in. He carried a pistol that pointed at Okura's heart.

"Mawembe?" Dave growled.

I shook my head and made the introductions.

"We missed you at the airport," Dave said.

"Yes. Very sorry for that but it could not be helped." Mawembe, he said, was being watched.

"By the army?" Dave asked.

Okura shook his head. He was a powerful looking man. His skin was brown, his eyes black and he had an enormous sloping forehead. He wore a blue two piece suit with flared trousers. The bulge in his inside jacket pocket was ill-concealed and made the garment hang badly. "No. Not the army. The P.S.U."

Dave lifted an eyebrow. He knew what the P.S.U. was, but I didn't. "What is the P.S.U.?" I asked.

"The Public Safety Unit," the Ugandan replied. "Amin's personal bodyguard." He spat out the words.

"They're not unlike the Tonton Macoutes of Haiti," Dave explained. "Heard of them, Mike?"

I nodded. "Papa Doc's boys."

"Well, here they are the Public Safety Unit and they're Idi's boys and they're poison. Do they still wear golf hats and reflecting sunglasses, Mr Okura?"

"They do. They are most horrible people."

"So how do we meet with Mawembe?"

"This is why I have come. To arrange a meeting place."

"Can't he come here?" I asked.

Okura shook his head. "Not here, no. Up there," he pointed to the ceiling, "is favourite place for . . er . . those in authority." We looked at him blankly. "Up where?" Dave asked.

"Up on the top floor of the hotel. The Coconut Grove Night Club. It is most popular with the P.S.U. and the army."

"We're living under a nightspot," I marvelled.

Dave frowned. "If we hear it we move downstairs," he said. "The hotel looks anything but full."

"So where do we meet, then?" I asked.

Okura looked about him and then whispered, "The Old Kampala Hill. Do you know it?"

When we shook our heads our visitor produced from a side pocket a folded piece of paper. He spread it flat on the bed and pointed. "There: the Old Kampala Hill. The summit. Tomorrow after dark, at seven o'clock. My sister's brother will meet with you. I leave the map with you."

"Right," Dave said. "Is it still possible to hire a car in Kampala?"

The black man nodded. "There are some left - and not many tourists to take them. See!" Again he pointed to the map. "There is the Kampala Road. And there. There is a garage where you may rent a car."

"Can't we get the hotel to hire us one?"

"You get better car there on Kampala Road. My brother. It is his place. And now I must go. Goodbye."

We bade him farewell and walked out on to the veranda. Five minutes later he appeared on the street below. Then he was gone.

"Well that's it for tonight," I remarked. I had had an idea. One to which I did not think Dave would take too kindly; one which it soon became apparent had also occurred to him.

"Yes, Mike, that's it for tonight. That's it *all* for tonight."

"What do you mean?" I asked innocently.

"I mean it's bedtime, Mike."

"What else?"

"It is *not* night club time, Mike."

"Certainly not."

"That's all right then. Get a good night's sleep. We'll need all our wits about us tomorrow."

"Goodnight, Dave."

He disappeared along the balcony. I heard his door slide shut and I tried not to think about coconut groves. Like a good boy I undressed, showered and got into bed. But I couldn't sleep. I tried counting hundred pound notes again and this might have done the trick if it had not been for the music. It started up at about eleven o'clock. It was soft music - well, soft by the time it had wafted through from the top floor - and incredibly seductive. It seemed to say, 'Come softly to me'. I fought it for a long time but it was no use. I slipped out of bed and outlined my rationale for disobeying orders. *I couldn't sleep, Dave - the damned music you know, and so I thought I would just nip upstairs and tell - ask - them to cut down the noise. No harm in that, was there? No. What was that, Dave? Who is she? Er, a refugee from that brute Amin. Met her upstairs. Needed a place to stay to escape from the Tonton Macoutes, so, naturally . . .*

I grinned with anticipation. I dressed quickly - casual but smart - and quietly let myself out of the room. I crept past Dave's door and took the stairs to the top floor two at a time. The sound of music grew louder. I edged along the corridor and there it was: Aladdin's cave, the Coconut Grove. The man on the door - the same one who had taken possession of our passports - treated me to a huge sneer and held the door open for me. The noise level doubled and I stopped momentarily. Then, bracing myself, I entered the nightclub.

The Coconut Grove was dark and jumping. The room consisted of a series of alcoves, each with its own imitation palm tree, and a larger, central space: the dance floor. The music was provided by a band of colourfully dressed Africans who swayed and sweated and sang to, alternately, western pop tunes and wild, repetitive, music that I learned later was Congolese. The dancers were, without exception, black. The girls were dressed in modern, western dress, flashy and provocative, while their partners were mainly young and wore coloured shirts and slacks. The smell was sweet, the feel was sticky and I almost left there and then. If only I had.

The bar was set up in one of the alcoves. I headed for it. By the time I reached it I had had my testicles fondled three times (each) and my bottom pinched twice. The first time it happened I was amazed and outraged: amazed because I am not used to being groped and outraged because I imagined the groper to be some pretty boy after my body. It was not. The first clutcher - and the subsequent ones - were pretty, vivacious girls with gleams in their eyes and gentleness in their fingertips. When I recovered from my shock, I smiled to myself. *Play your cards right, King, and you could get laid tonight!*

I ordered a beer and leaned sideways on the counter so that I could survey the scene and pick out the lucky girl. A tall, very black man moved from down the bar and stood by my side. I wondered who he was. The crocodile feeder, perhaps? Or the food tester to the President?

"You know where I can get white woman?"

I knew he was talking to me, but I didn't let on. I sipped my beer and leched away quietly.

"You know where I can get white woman?"

His voice had risen in pitch and I sensed that he was getting a bit excited. I thought of trying the old "I beg your pardon, are you talking to me?" routine, but I decided against it. "I'm sorry," I replied plaintively, "but I've just arrived in Uganda and I don't know any women yet - white or black."

He looked me up and down and I held my breath. This was one mean looking hombre. He glowered for a moment and then, suddenly, he smiled and the sun came out.

"When you arrive in beautiful Kampala?" he enquired.

"This evening."

"You not waste some time to find for fuckee-fuckee."

"Fuckee-fuckee? Oh yes. I mean no. You see I'm staying in the hotel and I heard the music - "

"This best night club in Uganda - in Africa! I know. I been in them all." He paused.

"Well. I'm glad I've come to the best one," I said lamely,

"I buy you drink. What you want?"

"Er, I'll have a Bell, thanks."

My companion called to the bartender by name and ordered a Bell beer and a large Scotch and soda for himself. While he waited to be served I looked *him* up and down. He wore a pale blue suit with bell-bottoms. I thought that bell-bottoms had gone out of fashion, but they still seemed to be all the rage in Uganda. His shirt was green and flowery; his shoes white. He was an ugly son-of-a-bitch with a wide nose and good teeth. I wondered what he did for a living.

"I am major in Army," he declared proudly. I

wondered if he could read minds as well. He passed me my drink and raised his own in salutation. "Cheers," he said.

"Cheers," I echoed. And what now? I thought.

"I never had white woman."

"Oh, well," I commiserated, "they're not all that . . . er . . different from your own . . . er . . "

"I never know till I try," he grinned. "When you are here long time, you get me white woman, O.K.?"

"Why . . .er . . I . . I'll try, of course."

Prevaricate, King. That's what you're good at. "I'll certainly see what I can do for you. Are there many white women left in Uganda?"

He grinned again and shrugged his shoulders. "I no think so. But that no matter. I only want one white woman. Any one will do."

I looked at him with horror. Charming, I thought. The swine!

"Why you come to Uganda?"

The nosey swine!

I explained that I was a doctor and that I had come to Kampala to visit with a fellow doctor who worked at Makerere University. "We are writing a book together and it was more convenient for me to visit Africa than for him to return, at this time, to the U.K.." I waited for him to ask what the book was about, but his disinterest was plain; he was probably thinking about a white woman. In the meantime, however, he was going to make do with one of his own colour because he laid down his glass and made a bee-line for a big woman with enormous breasts who was about to leave the dance square. He whisked her back on to the floor and disappeared with her into the melee of writhing bodies.

I finished my drink and considered getting the hell out of there. But then I saw her. She was standing by the wall that separated the bar from the next alcove and she was looking directly at me. She was about five foot three and black as the ace of spades. She wore a pink top which tried unsuccessfully to restrain wonderfully rounded breasts and a pair of black leather hot pants that bulged hips and spawned the shapeliest legs I have seen outside of Playboy magazine. She had come-to-bed eyes and a wide, white smile. She was gorgeous and I wanted her.

I smiled back and held out my arms in an invitation to trip the light fantastic. She nodded and we met at the edge of the dance floor where the band was playing "Blue Moon". To say that we danced would be to mislead. We gyrated; we were practically one right there in the middle of the dance floor. That little lady let her body do her talking and I responded predictably. But then things started to fall apart.

The first indication that something was wrong came from the girl. Suddenly she stiffened. Her pelvis unglued itself from mine and she took a step backwards, her face a study in surprise and dismay. She was looking past me at something or someone. I whirled round in time to catch an enormous fist as it bore into my nose and tried to flatten it. It flattened me. Tears of pain and anger blinded me and I shook my head to rid it of stars that had suddenly speckled my vision. I tried to get up, but decided that if I did so it would only be a temporary adjustment - the owner of the fist stood over me and dared me to move.

"White pig!" he hissed.

I stared at him. His mouth was twisted with hate that was all directed at me. The girl stood sullenly at his side. They were part of a ring of people who had converged on the action. I felt hated by all. However, when I made no move to retaliate - to get up even - they began to disperse - even Joe Louis, who departed with a sneer on his face. Of course I should have thrashed the swine, but I had held back, conscious that enough attention had been focussed on me already. *So that's how it was, Dave,* I rehearsed. *Had to force myself to stay put. God knows what damage I would have done the fellow if I hadn't -*

Wait a minute, King, you can't tell Dave! You're not supposed to be here! Oh, right enough.

I rose slowly to my feet. There was blood on the floor and on my shirt. Plop. There was now more blood on my shirt. I dug my handkerchief from my pocket and used it to staunch the flow. Boy, my nose was sore. I lurched in the direction of the sign that said 'toilets' and disappeared thankfully from view of the dance floor.

What a mess! Even when I cleaned off the blood it was obvious that some surgery had been attempted on my nose. *What happened to your face, Mike?* Dave would ask. *You fell out of bed? Fell from the verandah? Fourteen storeys? Oh, only thirteen. That's not so bad. No other injuries? Wow! What a man! There'll be a medal in this for you, boy.*

The bleeding stopped. I wiped my shirt with some toilet paper but the dark spots were there for good. The pain from my nose was excruciating, but it had cooled the ardour in my savage breast and groin and all I wanted now was to get out of that place and return to my own room. I checked in the mirror to see that the bleeding had not restarted. My nose looked twice and felt three times its normal size but it bled no more. I opened the toilet door and promptly closed it again.

I braced myself against the door but they opened it in three seconds flat. There were four of them. The leader was Joe Louis. His cronies looked equally hostile and I knew that they were not there merely to relieve themselves. There was one other thing that I noticed about them that I had missed on the dance floor: they were all wearing or carrying dark sunglasses.

I had just fallen foul of the Tonton Macoutes.

CHAPTER 7

I felt a fear that was to stay with me for a long time. It started deep in the pit of my stomach and radiated its debilitating effects to my legs which were rendered jellylike, to my heart which started to beat like a pneumatic hammer and to my mouth from which all salivary juices fled in panic. That it stopped short of relaxing my sphincter muscle was, I suppose, something to be thankful for.

While Joe Louis remained on guard by the door, his three lieutenants fanned out until I was surrounded. They were all smiling now and they rocked back and forth on their heels in some ritualistic motion that might, I thought, precede the kill. Desperately trying to remember Beresford's karate training, I raised my arms, extended my fingers and palms until they became cutting edges, and froze in a crouched position of readiness; whereupon my assailants to left and right approached and coolly gripped me by tricep and wrist and lifted me a foot from the floor. Just before I was able to kick out to back and front a hard object was rammed into the small of my back and a sixth sense told me that if I moved I was a dead man.

Why? I screamed silently.   Why? Surely not just   for dancing with that little trollop outside? We had only been *dancing* for God's sake!   Why then? Perhaps she was his wife! Or, worse, his mistress! Or worse, his sister! I'd heard that in some places a chap can be most protective of the virtue of his sister - especially when a bride price was involved (nobody wants damaged goods, do they?).

There's one thing about terror: it speeds up mental processes. All these thoughts and imaginings took only a fraction of a second. No sooner had the gun - it had to be a gun - been jammed into my spine, than the leader rasped, "You come with us quietly or you never leave this room alive. OK, msungu?"

I nodded. Msungu: wanderer, but really, white man. This was sounding more and more like the man didn't want his sister to have a bit of white. The two heavies on my flanks lowered me back to the floor. The bossman opened the door and led the way from the toilets, the five of us in single file with me piggy in the middle. When we were back in the dance area we formed a cross; I was grasped by both elbows and fairly rushed out of the Coconut Grove.

In the lift, when we passed floor fourteen, I felt like screaming "Dave", but I preserved my dignity and remained silent. I was hustled across the foyer with the empty animal cases and I wondered if, some day soon, I would take my place beside the zebra on the wall. Nobody saw us or, if they did, they felt no call to interfere. My escorts propelled me to the car park where I was bundled into the back of a big black Mercedes. Conversations sprang up but no remarks were addressed to me. I listened   carefully, but there was only one fact of which I was sure: the language spoken was not English.

The more I tried to rationalise my plight the more I came to the conclusion that the reason for my abduction was trivial. There was no way that these men of the P.S.U. could have known that I was a real live mercenary soldier. No, it was either due to the colour of my skin or to the fact that I had dared to dally with little black-eyed Suzie back there at the International. Or, more likely, a combination of the two.

I wondered where they were taking me. Perhaps I was to be held to ransom. I wondered how much I was worth. To my ex-wife, precisely nothing. To my Government? I hadn't a clue. It was surely more likely that my captors would just throw me in jail overnight, fine me a few thousand shillings in the morning and send me on my chastened way. How little I understood of the mentality of the members of General Amin's select band!

"Where are you taking me?" I asked.

"Shut up, fat pig-swine!" the chap on my right said.

I saw red. Pig-swine was O.K., but there was no way that I would take the "fat" slur lying down. I took a deep breath and blurted out as quickly as I could without sacrificing clarity: "I am not fat! But I am a friend of the Scotsman who taught your President Amin to box." (I was too: I had met the guy in a pub once in Edinburgh and I remembered that old Idi once referred to himself as the "last King of Scotland".) Then I slid lower in my seat and waited for the hand of retribution to form a fist and clatter me one. When it did I was neither surprised nor disappointed, but I had made my point; whether or not those morons understood me was their lookout. We drove for about fifteen minutes. It was a lovely night for a kidnapping.

When we finally came to a stop it was in front of a red and white boom that barred our way. A face appeared at the driver's window. Its owner spoke to my sparring partner in a language I did not understand and leered at me in a way that I did. Still chuckling, the soldier stepped back and I saw him motion for the boom to be lifted. As our car glided into the compound the driver turned to me and bade me welcome to Makindye Prison.

For four nights and three days (I think) I was locked up in a cell eight feet by seven. All I saw of another human being was a hand that, once a day, pushed a bowl of slops through the door. My cell boasted neither window nor toilet. Its stench did not improve with age, but I soon got used to the smell. Although I did not realise it at the time, it was on a Wednesday that they took me from the cell and marched me, naked, into the larger cellar that festered in the bowels of Makindye Jail.

The game of dominoes was well under way by the time I arrived.

CHAPTER 8

All I could do was stare at the man and his hammer. I was petrified. I understood at that moment something of the plight and resignation of Hitler's victims as they queued quietly to take their final shower. There was no-one to appeal to; no superior court to commute a sentence from one of death; no benevolence from which to expect mercy. This was despair. Without a wringing of hands; without a flood of tears; without an entreaty for clemency. There was no point. This was the end.

But first I was to be a murderer. I was to execute domino number eleven and then someone - it didn't matter who - would do me to death in the same way. I had already watched ten men die. All but one had breathed their last seconds after they had introduced one of their fellows to his Maker. Had they been murderers before? Surely not - not all of them anyway. But they had killed nevertheless, killed with what seemed an ease that I would never have credited had I not witnessed it with my own eyes.

I stretched out my arm and grasped the sledgehammer. It felt surprisingly light. Perhaps I had underestimated my own strength for all those years. Or perhaps the closeness to extinction is accompanied by a final burst of energy, just as a candle flares up before it dies . . .

Don't be ridiculous, King!

What do you mean?

You never actually held the hammer; you gripped it on the way down. You fainted, didn't you?

Overcome by the smell of blood and death!

You fainted.

O.K.. So I fainted. So what?

So it probably saved your life.

Well, that's good, isn't it?

Mmmm.

I don't know whether or not domino number eleven survived as well. I have no reason to believe that he did. Later I heard the little rhyme that was recited around Amin's Uganda; it suggested that he died like the rest:

"If you're white, you're all right;

If you're brown, stick around.

But if you're black! Oh, brother !

When I came to I was in darkness and I was lying on my back on a cold, unyielding surface. My head throbbed - I must have struck it when I fell - but I didn't mind the pain - I was alive, wasn't I? Slowly and carefully I struggled to my feet and, with arms outstretched, inched forward blindly to explore my new enclosure. Eight feet by seven. I had been here before.

I was still naked and thankful that this was not Siberia - if anything, I was too warm. I edged to one corner of the cell and sat down gingerly. I wondered how my reprieve had come about, why I was still alive.

I remained undisturbed in my private room for several hours. I tried to relax, but my mind was too full of recent horrors and my body could find no comfort on the hard floor of the cell.

One domino, two domino, three domino, four;

Five domino, six dom; can stand this no more!

I got up and paced up and down only to find that the rhythm lodged in my head was not easily eradicated.

One step, two step, three step, four;

Five step, six, run out of floor.

I sat down again.

You know what's happened, don't you?

It was the voice of my left shoulder.

No, I don't.

(The voice of my right shoulder.)

It's perfectly obvious.

Go on then.

They've rumbled you.

Who've rumbled us?

The Tonto en Croutes.

The Tonton Macoutes?

Correct.

How could they have rumbled us - we've scarcely arrived in this God-forsaken country.

I don't know how they've done it, but that's the only solution. They've realised that you are a spy and a mercenary and a potential assassin.

So why didn't they just carry out the

execution?

Elementary, my dear King. That execution was merely for being white and for messing with one of the boys' girl friends; a quiet execution was appropriate. But, for the triple offence of spying, mercenarying and murder, a public hanging is what is called for.

That's what you think?

Elementary, don't you think?

You know what I think?

What?

I think that you should fuck off.

Oh, charming.

I thought you'd like that.

We lapsed into silence and I searched for other explanations for my change of circumstances that had a happier ending. Like the cavalry had arrived. With John Wayne. Talking of whom, I wondered what Dave Mercouri was doing. What would he have thought when he found out that I had vanished? He wouldn't have been too pleased. He would have had to meet with Mawembe alone without me to hold his hand. That wouldn't have bothered him, but not knowing my whereabouts would have caused him no little annoyance. Would he have aborted the mission? Surely not. He would probably have left the International Hotel though so that he could not be traced there from information I might divulge. Cheeky bastard! As if I would betray him! Where would he have gone? Mawembe, I suppose, would have advised him.

Perhaps Snyder and the rest had made their landing. Perhaps it was all over. Hardly successful if that were so because, had I not just seen in the cellar the target of their operation? Maybe they were all dead. Maybe they had been captured and were on their way now to visit me. A thought occurred to me - one that was as horrible as the sights and scenes of my previous experience. Suppose this cell, this . . eight by seven, was to be home to all, including . . . Jean Marc! Horror of horrors! Quick! Change the subject, King!

I wondered how Sue Dailly was. Lovely Sue Dailly with whom I had spent delightful hours in the Seychelles. And Yvonne. Yvonne, the chambermaid at the Sunset Hotel. Yvonne who had, probably, given me a dose: the same dose I had handed on to the lovely Sue. She hadn't been so lovely when she had accused me, in front of everybody at the Sunset Hotel, of being a liar, a cheat and an adulterer - and pox-ridden to boot! Change the subject, King. Think of something nice - one of the good times in your life.

I was stumped.

Surely there was *one* time?

One domino, two domino, three domino, four
. . . .

I felt sick. Was I just dreaming? Had it all been a nightmare? I knocked my head - gently on the wall but I did not wake up. This was no dream.

CHAPTER 9

When Dave woke up the morning after my disappearance the sun was shining and he was hungry. He explained later what had happened to him during the days of my incarceration. When he heard my plan to go into print he said that he wanted to write his bit for himself. I had to promise him that I would not change his copy.

I picked up the phone by my bedside and dialled next door.   There was no reply. Thinking that Mike was sitting on the john I heaved myself out of bed, slipped   a towel around my waist and slid open the glass door of the balcony that connected with his room.   His room was empty. Like his head.

Where had that dumb limey got to? Out jogging? Not a chance! At breakfast? That was a possibility. I hustled back to my own room, got dressed and went downstairs in search of food and Mike King. The first was easy. Orange juice out of a tin, toast and instant coffee - ugh! But of King there was no sign. I checked at reception in case he had gone for a morning constitutional and maybe left a message there. Fat chance.

I went back to my room and began to worry. Where was he? My gut told me that he was in trouble. I wondered if he had, after all, paid a visit to the night spot on the roof. Go up and see. Maybe he's still there. I climbed to the fifteenth floor. The 'Coconut Grove' was all that there was up there. It smelled. Of stale cigarette smoke and booze and unwashed bodies. All the bodies were long gone. I went back to my room and began to worry in earnest.

Fact number one: King was missing. Fact number two: I was - we were - to meet with Mawembe in a few hours time. Had Mike been arrested? Or was he just shacked up with some chick in a corrugated iron hut in a Kampala suburb? Fact number three: if he wasn't out whoring, then I was no longer safe in the International Hotel. If Mike had got himself arrested then he was going to finger me. He wouldn't mean to. But he would talk.

My passport. Better get that. I returned to reception. The big broad with the classy chassis was on duty.

"I was told to collect my passport this morning - Dave Stavros," I told her. She smiled and asked me to wait. When she reappeared she had them both - mine and Mike's. I took them, thanked her and went back upstairs for a final check of the fourteenth floor. No King. I collected essentials from my valise, disposed them about my person, and got the hell out of the hotel.

The sun was already high when I walked out into the city. Everywhere was green. Lawns and parks, once tidy, sprawled all around and lent a beauty to Kampala that her dilapidated buildings tried to deny. And it was quiet. Where the hell was everybody?

I needed wheels and so I headed for the Kampala Road and Okura's brother's place. I walked as far as the Grand Hotel and there stopped for a coffee. I needed some more time to think. I decided against the Kampala Road garage. Better to rent a car from someone we didn't know. Operate on the 'need to know' principle. Especially now that Mike was missing.

I made enquiries at the hotel reception and, for an exorbitant sum, paid in dollars, I rented a Fiat two door with a broken side window and bald tyres. It was the best they had. I also picked up a map of the city and drove off - chugged off more like - to reconnoitre the Old Kampala Hill.

The grassy knoll was one of many hills in the city. It was a good place for a meet because from the top any climbers could be spotted long before they became a physical threat - unless, of course, they happened to be snipers armed with rifles and *telescopic sights. Our information was that Amin's army was not all that well equipped. The story also was that its soldiers were poor shots. Seems like I remember somebody saying the same about Lee Harvey Oswald!*

I circled the place a few times, decided on where I would leave the car later and headed back downtown for something to eat. Pizza at the Speke Hotel filled the gap that had grumbled. I sipped a Tusker beer and worried some more about King.

When I finished eating I rang his room at the International just in case he had merely stepped out and was now returned. No reply. Stupid limey. For all his faults, however, I had grown fond of Mike. I hoped he hadn't gottnt himself into too much trouble.

I toured in and around Kampala for a couple of hours and liked the city. It was a pity it had fallen on such hard times. At 6 o'clock I headed back to the Old Kampala Hill. It was time for the meet.

I slid the Fiat into the parking area belonging to a school that stood close to the Hill. The Old Kampala Senior Secondary School it was called. I crossed the road and walked to the top of the Hill. A man was waiting there. I recognised him from a photograph back in England. It was Mawembe. He was a well built guy with very black skin and greying hair. He wore a fawn safari suit and brown shoes. His handshake was firm, his eyes steady. I showed him a half Ugandan shilling and he matched it with the other half. It was better than using a password. Passwords make me want to laugh.

"Mawembe," he said.

"Stavros," I replied.

"And Dr King?"

"I don't know."

He stared at me for some moments. "You . . . don't know?"

I shook my head and shrugged.

"Mr Stavros. You arrive here only yesterday. And you lose Dr King already? How is this possible?"

I shrugged again. Just lucky, I thought. Aloud I told him what had happened: that Mike had been in his room last night but not this morning.

"This could be very dangerous for us," Mawembe said.

"I know. I've quit the hotel. If he is captured he might talk. He knows your name too. I'm sorry."

He looked away over the city and I could see that he was a worried man. Then he shrugged. He was also a realist, was Dr Mawembe. "What do you say?" he asked. "The milk she is spilled. We must plan accordingly. You are right to leave the hotel. I too shall move my base until the . . . thing is done."

It was back to business. Mawembe told me where Snyder would parachute in. It was a place called Namulonge, a mile or so off the main road connecting Kampala and Entebbe. Amin was due to be at his HQ at Entebbe for the next week at least. He liked to move around, but he had just arrived at the Lake and the chances were that he would stay there a few days.

"What is this place, Namulonge?" I asked.

"It is - or was - a research station for agriculture. It is abandoned now for six months or more. It is suitable."

I took his word for it.

"I shall contact my people. They are ready. They can be here soon."

"Good. Where will you go?" he asked.

"Where do you recommend?"

"It is better you will come with me. To Jinja.

We have many friends there. It will not be long and the madman will be dead." He spat on the ground. "Now. You will come with me. You have a car?"

"Yes. "

"Leave it. We shall go in my car to Jinja."

And we did.

****

Jinja is the second largest city in Uganda and lies about fifty miles from Kampala. It's a real nice place. There's a big dam there - the Owen's Falls Dam - and a hydroelectricity plant. Mawembe drove me to a nice big ranch-house type building overlooking the lake. We went inside and he introduced me to two men. One was called Ben, the other Otiambo. I wasn't told their last names and I didn't ask what they were. They had news from Kampala which they broke to Mawembe in Swahili. They didn't know that I speak Swahili and I didn't let on.

When Mawembe relayed the message to me he made some changes which, at another time I might have found funny. The "stupid English fool" in Swahili translated to "your English friend" and the "fat foreign sex-maniac" became "your . er . fun-

loving comrade". The message, however, was unequivocal. King had been picked up by the Public Safety Unit and was being held at Makindye Prison.

"Where was he captured?" I asked. It was important to know. If Mike had been lifted from his hotel room then we were blown. If, on the other hand . . .

"In the Coconut Grove Nightclub at the International Hotel."

The son-of-a-bitch!

"Do you know why they took him?"

Ben nodded. He explained in broken English that his cousin had been in the nightclub the evening before and had seen the whole thing. The stupid Msungu, apparently, had made a pass at the girl friend of one of the P.S.U.. There had been a fight - one-sided - and Mike had been hustled out of the hotel by a group of heavies. Ben's cousin overheard one of then say that the only date King would have was with a sledgehammer in Makindye.

"So they don't know to connect him with our little....... party."

"No. Not as long as he does not volunteer the information."

"Mike wouldn't do that."

"You are sure?"

" We - e - ell," I muttered, "he ain't big on volunteerin'."

"He has been most irresponsible," Mawembe said.

I surprised myself by starting to defend Mike. "He's new at the game - he's got a lot to learn."

"Then let us hope, my friend, that the price of his education is not our heads."

It was a sobering thought.

No less so than my next one which I aired aloud - to the puzzlement and then dismay of my companions.

"We'll have to spring him. Get him out."

They looked at me as if I was nuts. Mawembe told me why. He spoke gently as if to a child.

"Mr Stavros. Your friend is not in the . . er . . local jail. He is held in Makindye Military Prison. At any one time there are as many as two hundred soldiers garrisoned there. An escape attempt is out of the question. Besides, we cannot jeopardise our

mission. Perhaps after that has been accomplished - and your friend is still alive - we shall be able to free him."

Poor Mike. Hang on in there, boy, I thought. I wondered if I would ever see him again alive.

CHAPTER 10

A long time later I heard the bolts being drawn back. The door creaked open and a black hand appeared. It placed on the floor a plate and a cup. The plate contained a mound of stuff that looked like custard and the cup was three quarters full. The food was matoke, the staple food of Ugandans: boiled green bananas. I didn't like it - it was very bland - but I wolfed it down. I was starving and would have scoffed poached python if that had been offered instead. The matoke didn't fill me, but it went some way to assuaging the hunger pangs from which I had been suffering. The cup contained tepid water, presumably neither filtered nor boiled. I drank it down as if it had been a cheeky little Frascati served in a crystal glass on the outskirts of Rome itself. I hoped that the inoculations I had had against cholera and yellow fever were effective.

I had just finished licking my plate when my first visitor was shown in. He didn't recognise me but I recognised him.

"Whit a fuckin' shite-house!" he growled. Then: "Who the fuck are you?" when I coughed to announce my presence. He peered at me in the near darkness and I looked at him, but all we could see were silhouettes.

"Are you a fuckin' darkle?" he rasped. I muttered incoherently in reply; some sixth sense warned me not to declare myself - not yet anyway.

"Christ! A fuckin' dummy! They've locked me up wi' a fuckin' dummy! Hey you! Kin ye no' speak fuckin' English?"

"Mimi nataka chakula," I said. It was the only full sentence in Swahili I knew and I used it to buy time to think. I had told him that I was hungry - he was a cook, wasn't he? - but he didn't quite get the message.

"Christ! A Kraut! They've locked me up wi' a fuckin' darkie Kraut!"

I sat down with my back to the wall and watched him as he explored the cell.

One step, two step, three step, four . . .

He muttered constantly to himself as he paced. I strained to make out what he was saying - it may have concerned me - but it was hopeless. The only words I could make out for sure were "fuck" or its present participle. I was about to declare myself when he suddenly strung two words together that I could make out.

"Fuckin' bastard!"

I went cold. In the baking heat of our little cell I went cold. The hairs on the back of my neck crawled to attention. I knew - I don't know how, I just knew - that he was referring to me. What had happened out there? I had to find out.

"Oo are you, mein fren'," I said in my British impression of a German speaking English. (If the Gallopping Gourmet thought I was a Gerry, then why not act the part?)

"Eh?"

"I ask oo you are."

"Oh, do ye now? Ah'm Bonnie Prince Cherlie. Who the fuck are you?"

" . . er . . Ich bin Deutcher."

"Whit are ye daein' here?"

"I am ein captif."

"Ah kin see that, Jimmy, but whit huv ye done?"

Inspiration struck.

"I try to . . . how you say? . . . blow up President Amin. I fail." I imagined a gleam of interest in the little cook's eye; it was manifested in his voice.

"Did ye now?" he said. "I'n't that a coincidence?"

"A coincidence?"

"Yeah. We tried tae bump him off an' a', but we were selt doon the river."

I caught my breath.

"Zie vere . . betrayed?" I gasped.

"Aye," he rasped. "By a bastard who calls hissel' a Geordie . . "

Oh, no, I thought.

" . . an' a doctor tae boot!"

Oh God!

"What happened?" I croaked.

He was silent for a while. Then he said, ""How d'ah ken you're no' a spy?"

"A spy? Oo?   Me? I tell you. I am captif - like you!"

"Ach, ah suppose it disnae really matter anyway.   They caught us red-handed - we were jumpin' oot o' the sky at the time.

"You are parashooters?" I asked.

"Ye could say that. Anyway, we landed in this field - at night - and suddenly it was day. They must've had a thousand searchlights on us. It wis like Hampden Park wi' Celtic an' Rangers playin'. And then they started tae shoot. Millions o' the black bastards wi' machine guns. And they mowed us doon."

"Who else escaped?" I blurted out. I heard his sharp intake of breath. I realised why. I had used my normal voice. I waited.

"Whit the fuck is this?" he said slowly. He stopped pacing and swung round to face in my direction. His five and a half feet towered over me. As I struggled to my feet I could almost hear his brain whirr into top gear as he strove to identify me. Then, in the gloom, light dawned.

"You!" he hissed.

He lunged at my throat without warning. I grabbed his shoulders and tried to hold him off. (There is a very big difference between grappling with another naked man and wrestling with a willing, seductive woman. What do you do with your legs for example? Or your groin for God's sake?) When he discovered that he wasn't managing to strangle

103

me he decided to give me a Glasgow kiss. This manoeuvre requires no backswing: the forehead is simply thrust forward and shatters its target, the opposition nose bridge. I was lucky. As his head came forward I happened to step back in an effort to get some wall purchase. He was in mid air - I'm six feet remember - when I hit the wall. I kicked out as I did so and I felt my knee come to a sudden stop as it angled into his crotch. He screamed in pain.

He fell to the floor and writhed in agony. Not a happy little Glaswegian cook, I thought. But he would soon recover and I shuddered to think the form his vengeance would take. I had to immobilise him and yet, understandably, I was loathe to try and pin him to the floor by lying on top of him. So I planked my foot on his neck and screamed, "I didn't betray you - and I can prove it!" I felt his Adam's apple against my big toe. "Promise to behave and I'll let you up."

"A' right! A' right!" he gargled. "But let me go!"

I lifted my foot and tensed in case he changed his mind about behaving, but all he did was slide down against the wall and, sitting, began to massage his private parts. He groaned. I also sat down, as far away as possible from him, and started to talk. I told him the truth - the unexpurgated version - there didn't seem to be any point in lying. I may have changed some emphases - like stressing that the only reason I had gone to the Coconut Grove in the first place was to complain about the noise - but his sceptical snort dissuaded me from further romanticising. When I recounted the scene in the dungeon I felt sick. I sensed that he was impressed, but it took him no more than a few seconds to spot the flaw.

"So how come ye didnae get yer heid bashed in an' a'?" he asked. He stopped playing with himself and I prepared myself for another attack. It did not, however, come. My honest reply must have rung true. Either that or his balls were sorer than I had thought.

"I don't know," I said. "I just don't know."

We sat in silence for a minute.

"Heck," I said at last.   He grunted. "How come you're so sure that it was me who tipped them off?"

"We were telt."

"We?"

"Aye. After the debacle o' the landin' some o' us managed tae fight our way through the bastards' lines. Ah found masel' wi' the Colonel an' Beresford. We hid in the balcony o' a squash court. It wis one

105

o' them open ones - nae roof, ye unnerstand. We climbed in. Later we heard them tryin' the door but it wis locked and they went away - didnae think o' lookin' up, did they?

"We heard some o' them talkin' - in Swahili. Captain Beresford kin speak Swahili. They were sayin' how well everything had gone - how Amin wis safe an' how most o' the mercenaries had been shot or captured. They were sayin' how grateful they were for the tip off. Frae the English doctor!"

I shuddered.

"Snyder couldnae credit it - an' neither could I at the start - but Beresford said he wis sure that's what they said. We stayed up there till things were quiet an' then we climbed doon again. Snyder figured that we should head for the Kenyan border so we struck oot east, keepin' off the roads as much as possible.

"Well, after a few miles we got split up. Then it got light and ah walked intae a patrol. That wis about two hours ago. They brought me here."

I listened in horror to the little man's story. It was clear now what had happened - clear, at any rate, to me.

CHAPTER 11

"If only Mercouri were here," I muttered.

Heck sniffed. "Don'tcha think it's a wee bit too crowded in here already?" he said.

"He could prove it."

"Eh?'?

"Dave. He could prove that it wisnae - wasn't - me."

"Yeah? How?"

"Well, he knew that I didn't know where you were coming in - I never met Mawembe, remember. And if I didn't know that then I couldn't have laid on the reception committee."

"Big deal."

"You don't seem to care."

"Ah don't."

"Then you believe me?"

"It disnae matter a fuck, dis it?"

And I suppose he was right.

"We never saw Mercouri," Heck said.

"Well, that's good news, isn't it? I mean, if Dave didn't make it to the drop then he probably didn't get captured."

"An' you think he's goin' tae spring us outae here?"

"Well, he might."

"Dinnae hud yer breath."

We lapsed into silence and lost ourselves in our private thoughts. I wondered about Snyder and the others: McGurk and Jean-Marc and Beresford. I wondered the most about Beresford. How many of them were dead? How many captured?

I wondered why I wasn't dead.

I must have fallen deeply asleep because the next thing I was aware of was voices. At first I thought it was just Heck muttering to himself, but as my eyes began to re-focus I made out, not one, but two figures on the floor in the far corner of the cell.

"Who's that?" I challenged.

"Hello, Mike," one of the figures said, "you no-good, stupid, undisciplined, weak, ornery, son-of-a-bitch!"

I shrank against my wall at the ferocity of this, albeit verbal, attack. I had recognised Dave Mercouri's voice. "So they got you too, eh?" I said lamely.

"No," he growled, "I invited myself."

"What do you mean?"

It was Heck who answered. "It means he got hissel' arrested so that he could get us oot."

"Oh great!" I exclaimed. "Wonderful! So let's go. Everybody ready?" I stood up ready to punish Mercouri's vicious attack with all the sarcasm I could muster. Dave laughed. "Not yet, not yet," he said. I sat down again. Who was he kidding, I thought? They were going to try us in public and then they were going to hang us. That's what they were going to do.

"So you went upstairs," Dave said.

How did *he* know?

"Heck's been telling me (as least I think he has) about your adventures in the Coconut Grove - and afterwards. You tell him the truth?"

Cheeky sod!

I nodded yes.

"So he didn'ae ken where we were droppin'," Heck remarked.

"What's that again?" Dave asked.

"So he didnlae ken where we were droppin'."

"He's trying to say that I couldn't know the location of the drop site," I explained

"That's right. That's whit ah said."

"Of course you couldn't," Dave agreed. "I didn't know it myself until after you . . . disappeared."

"So what did you do?" I asked.

"I went to Jinja - with Mawembe. We stayed there till yesterday. Then we came west to meet up with Snyder and the boys. By the time we got near Namulonge the place was crawling with troops. We heard the shooting. We thought it was a wipe-out." He stood up.

One step, two step, three step . . . and that was as far as he could go: the cell had become awfully crowded.

"We managed to get away without being

seen and made it to Kampala. We holed up at Okura's place - Mawembe's brother-in-law, remember?"

I nooded in the gloom.

"Snyder was brought there this morning."

"Snyder!"

"Yes. He's wounded. It's bad."

And suddenly it all became clear - or so I thought. *Snyder's hurt so what does he need? A doctor! Where's the nearest doctor? Mawembi's a doctor but the wrong kind: Mawembe's a Doctor of Biochemistry. OK, so where's the next nearest medical doctor? He lives across the street, but both his sons asked for reflecting sunglasses for Christmas last year so we can't go there. Wonder where King got to?*

"How did you know where to find me?"

"Okura's brother-in-law."

"Mawembe!"

"No. On the other side. He's a soldier. He used to be stationed here."

"Here!"

"Yes."

"Can he be trusted?

"Apparently so. Anyway, he told Okura that some of the prisoners were being held here at Makindye and that one of them was a doctor. He thought that if a weapon could be smuggled in, there was a way out."

"So here you are."

"Here I am."

"And Snyder still needs a doctor."

"Oh no. We got him a doctor. He just needs some of his men saved, that's all. He's traumatised - and not just with bullet wounds."

"Oh. "

"Yes.

Silence.

"You mentioned a weapon . . . ? All I can see - well, not exactly *see* - what I mean is, you don't seem to be carrying a weapon other than . . . ."

He stopped pacing, stood side on to me and bent over. His hand went behind his back and he withdrew something from his backside that looked long and thin.

"What - ? "

He squatted and undid his slender parcel. "I don't suppose there's a john available," he said. I almost replied "no" but I stopped myself in time. He crumpled up something and dropped it in the corner.

"What is it?"

"It's a piece of wire - cunningly wrapped - well, it *was* wrapped - in greased paper."

"A piece of wire?"

"A garrotte."

"Ah."

"When do we eat?"

"Eat?"

"I assume they feed us."

"Oh yes. But I don't know when. Seems ages ago since the last time though." I explained how the hand would appear and shove the food through the door.

"How many?"

"How many what?"

"How many waiters?"

"I don't know. But I've only seen the one hand."

"OK. We'll have to assume that there'll be more than one. So this is what we do when they come a-callin'. He outlined his plan and assigned roles to Heck and me.

"According to Okuru," he went on, "there should be a guard room at the end of one of these corridors."

I nodded. "There is. At the end of *this* one. I've seen it. I've been *in* it - when they took me down to the dungeon."

"The stairs to the basement start in that guard room, correct?"

"That's right."

"Then that's where we've got to make for."

It sounded like another death sentence.

"Dave," I said quietly, "wild horses could not drag me back down to that cellar. Besides," I added, "when I was in the guard room I wasn't alone. Apart from my own personal escort, there were four other soldiers so even if you get that far, you're going to have problems."

The switch from "me" to "you" was not lost on Dave. "Mike," he said, "if Heck had been the only one in here, then I would have been happy to have tried the break just for him. However, you also are here. Now. That staircase is the only way out of this place for us. Beyond the dungeons is a door. It leads to a tunnel. The tunnel leads to the outside. You're going along that tunnel - with or without a length of wire tied round your scrotum."

I swallowed. Dave was getting a bit ahead of himself, but, at least, according to his plan, we wouldn't have to go *into* the cellar.

"Anyway," he continued, "we won't have to go *into* the cellar."

Heck had listened to all of this patiently, but evidently he thought that enough was enough. "If he disnae want to come, major, jest leave him," he suggested.

"He comes," Dave retorted. "Snyder said to bring everybody."

"Oh well, fair enough. But if 'e gets bolshie we might be better tyin' the wire round his balls."

This conversation had gone far enough. "All right. All right," I said. "There'll be no need for gratuitous violence - save it for our jailers. I suppose you've got the key to this door to the outside," I added sarcastically.

"No, Mike, I do not have the key. The key . . ." he paused for effect " . . . is on the back of the door. You see, visitors don't normally get that far alive. The tunnel is used to remove dead meat - to save stinking up the rest of the jail."

"The dead domino trail," I muttered.

"Huh?"

"The domino trail. I thought Heck told you my story."

I imagined Dave grinning in the dark. "He did. But I'm not sure that I got all the details. Why don't you run it by me one more time."

"Oh Gawd, no, again," Heck wailed.

Wire round the balls indeed! I'd make him suffer! I started at the beginning and told my dominoes-in-the-dungeon experience slowly. After I had finished - by now Heck was making loud snoring sounds - Dave said, "Christ! You were a lucky man!"

"It's been bothering me."

"Bothering you?"

"Yes. Why? Why did they not finish me off as well as those other wretches?"

"Ay, why?" demanded Heck. The little Glaswegian could not resist breaking possum.

"It's obvious why," Dave said.

I gawped. Had I missed something?

"Word must have come through about the Namulonge fiasco. Somebody would have put two and two together. You had to have been involved, Mike. So you were being saved for the public trial. And public execution."

"You think so?"

"Sounds reasonable, don't you think?"

"Uh-huh."

We all mulled over this for a while. Then Heck had a thought.

"Wis Captain Beresford no' at Okuru's?" he asked. "The three o' us were the gither till ah got lost."

"The three of you were . . . . ?" Dave echoed. "Oh yes. Were together. No, Beresford wasn't there."

"I bet he wasn't!" I said.

"You seem awful sure, Mike, for someone

117

who also wasn't there."

"You bet I'm sure! It was that slimy Welsh bastard who sold us down the river!"

"Who? Beresford? Come on now, Mike. I know that you two didn't exactly hit it off, but that's no reason to - "

"It had to be Beresford."

"Why?" Dave's voice was hard.

"Because . . . it wasn't me!"

"I don't follow."

"Heck. Tell Dave about the squash court."

"Ah already did. "

"Tell him again - and this time try it in English. I don't think he fully got the message before."

Heck sniffed, but he repeated the conversations around the squash court and, with me interpreting, Dave finally understood. "The dirty bastard," he breathed.

Even Heck saw it clearly now.

"The fuckin' - sorry, Major - the bluidy shite!"

"But why?" I wanted to know.

"Money?" Dave said. "What else?"

We fell silent again and I thought about traitors from Judas on. I was going to have Beresford - somehow I was going to have him because, not only had he sold us out, but he had also tried to pin the rap on me! The bastard! I wondered where he was now. I wondered how he would like a length of wire tied round his scrotum - or his balls!

We had to wait two hours before the food arrived. Then things happened so quickly that I'm not sure to this day if I've got the sequence correct.

CHAPTER 12

Sliding bolts sent us scuttling to our battle stations. Dave crouched behind the door with me right behind him; Heck stood at the other side of it, flat against the wall. The door opened a quarter and the plate appeared. Dave pounced. He grabbed the waiter's wrist and yanked while I simultaneously hauled the door fully ajar. As the warder's body hurtled into the cell, Heck leapt outside with the garrotte looped and ready for use.

Then the plan hiccupped. Instead of jumping to Heck's assistance outside, I found myself jammed between the open door and the wall. I only heard what happened next: the sound of fists crashing against bone and a muffled scream that gave birth to a horrible gargle. Then there was silence. I pushed the door to and looked around it. Dave was sucking the knuckles of his right hand while, with his left, he was trying to prise Heck from the outstretched body of a black man whose tongue stuck obscenely from lifeless lips. In the cell with me lay the first waiter. He was bleeding and unconscious.

Dave looked at me accusingly. "What if there

had been three?" he asked quietly. I muttered my apologies but he cut me short. "We'll have to be quick," he hissed. "He's about your size, Mike, and this one's clothes'll fit me."

We stripped the soldiers and climbed into their outer clothing. The material was rough and uncomfortable but Dave and I were lucky - Heck had to make do with a shirt. He reminded me of Jack Nicholson on his knees playing Wee Willie Winkie.

This way," Dave whispered. He had a map of the prison etched in his brain from Okura's cousin's sketches. If they were accurate we had only one fear: meeting any of a couple of hundred soldiers who might resent our leaving without saying goodbye. And if they weren't accurate, I knew the way.

At least we were now armed. Dave and Heck had commandeered the rifles of the fallen waiters; we weren't going down without a fight. The little Glaswegian pressed his garrotte into my hand. It was bloody. I shuddered and shook my head. He stuffed it into my tunic pocket.

The corridor was narrow and poorly lit, but it was blessedly empty. We passed several other doors and Dave took time to peer through their Judas holes to see if any of our comrades were being held in separate cells. His expression, which became grimmer by the peek, told us there were not.

We reached the guard room and stopped. And listened. We waited. And listened. Until Heck lost patience and couldn't wait any longer.   "Aw fuck it!" he said out loud, a second before he kicked the door open and went in shooting.

Dave mouthed "Don't!" and my lips framed a "Please!", but we were too late. We heard a rifle bark three times. The shots reverberated against the walls of the room and almost deafened us in the corridor. I don't know if the three soldiers inside heard them but if they did they were in no condition to complain. When we looked, we saw that two of them had bleeding hearts and the other had developed a cyclopean eye where he used to have worry lines. Heck stood over his victims. He was picking his nose.

Again we waited. And listened. Somebody had heard the shots. He appeared up the stairs from the basement and Mercouri blew the top of his head off with a single shot. We didn't wait any longer.

"Come on," Dave ordered. He ran to the steps and, followed by Heck and then myself, raced down them. The corridor ahead was empty. We passed my cellar. I accelerated and almost collided with Heck.

"Hurry up!" I yelled.

We reached the end. I did collide with Heck. Guess what he said?

"Shut up, you two!" Dave commanded. Then he added,   "Got it!"

I heard a key being thrust into a lock. Metal ground on metal and a door protested at being flung open. Threads of thin yellow light from the basement corridor filtered part of the way down a tunnel. Beyond was darkness. Our bare feet smacked the stone floor as the gloom enveloped us. I held both my hands in front of me, knuckles forward in case I again collided with Heck.

At the same time as I saw a light ahead I also heard noises behind me. Voices. Belonging to people who did not sound too happy; I didn't doubt that we had knocked off somebody's cousin - or even brother-in-law.

"Hurry!" I gasped. "They're coming after us!"

The light ahead grew brighter. And then we were in the open, well, not exactly the open, but outside. We had emerged in the middle of a copse of trees. The moon was nearly full and cast shadows that threatened us but also gave us cover. The cover came from tree shadows, the threats from rough blocks of stone which were randomly dotted throughout the wooded area. We were in a cemetery; the dead meat didn't have far to travel before being shovelled to rest. I wondered who had supplied the headstones.

"This way!" Dave whispered. We ran across the burial ground and found ourselves on a road of hard-packed red dirt known locally as 'murram'.

"Whit bus d'we get?" Heck whispered.

Dave had the answer. "Not a bus," he said, "a taxi!"

Fifty yards down the road we could see the silhouette of a saloon car. Its engine was running. We raced towards it as rifle fire from behind us punctuated the farts that belched from the dilapidated Peugeot. We piled in the back and in no time were careering out of that infernal place. We had escaped.

CHAPTER 13

The journey that night was memorable - and nearly our last. There were three men in the car's front bench: Okura, whom I knew and Ben and Otiambo, Dave's pals from Jinja. Ben drove and I think that he was trying to run over every pothole in that track of potholes. The car's springs were shot - in fact, the only elasticity it had left was in its sides. It was, indeed a taxi, one of the type which, as the story goes, was involved in a horrendous collision with a daddy wart hog. The bad news was that, besides the unfortunate wart hog, ten people were killed outright. The good news was that the other dozen passengers survived.

Okura told us about the curfew that had been imposed immediately after our abortive landing: it was a twenty-four one and was to operate in Kampala, Entebbe and the countryside in between. He also described the roadblocks about ninety seconds before we hit the first one. It consisted of a sapling, recently cut, and stretched across the road between two forked sticks. It was guarded by about a dozen soldiers. The Peugeot smashed through the tree like a hatchet through a wishbone. The soldiers scattered and, from our little flying arsenal we peppered them with rifle fire from the rear and revolver bullets from the front seat. I managed to duck and keep my head out of the way of a salvo loosed by those soldiers who had managed to remain on their feet. A couple of bullets thudded into the car body and one screamed through the rear window but, miraculously, nobody was hit.

Okura turned to face us. Moonbeams picked out his big white teeth which lit up the centre of the car. "We very lucky fellows," he boomed. "On main road, roadblocks much better."

"Better?"

"Yes. Much better. Strips of steel with spikes this size - " he held up a gnarled thumb - "make sure that no car pass."

"Can we keep off the main roads all the way?" Dave asked.

Okura shook his head. "Not all the way. For last part of journey we leave car and walk. It is the only way."

We drove without lights for another mile or so and then Ben slowed down. He allowed the taxi to leave the track and nudged it into a large bush. We got out. Okura snapped an order to his two men who bent to the task of pushing the car further into the foliage. Dave and Heck joined the three Africans and, when the vehicle had almost disappeared, I too lent shoulder and grunt to push it out of sight.

We saw the next roadblock from the safety of a clump of banana trees. The main road lay across us and, just as Okura had said, a steel strip straddled the double lane. Its two inch spikes threatened to shred the tyres of any vehicle that ignored the warning sign of roadblock. The silhouettes of a large number of soldiers confirmed that this was not a spot at which to dally and so, with Okura in the lead, we crept, Indian file, deeper into the bush.

The lightest of breezes tapped our cheeks as we minced through the banana plantation. I learnt a lot of surprising things about bananas during and after that walk in the jungle. The plant, a gigantic herb springing from an underground stem, forms a false trunk that can rise to twenty feet. After it fruits it dies and is replaced by another arising from the underground stem. Desirable commercial bunches can weigh up to one hundred and fifty pounds and even for local consumption they are not allowed to ripen fully on the plant. Occasionally, however, one does and when this happens, it falls from the tree of its own accord.

One did just that as we skirted another murram track that would lead eventually to Okura's shamba. We heard it landing. Reflexively, we turned to see a couple of hundred bananas sliding off the head of a coal-black soldier who had been about to mow us down with his semi-automatic rifle. I don't know if the bananas broke his neck, but by the time Heck had bludgeoned him with the stock of his own weapon, the extent to which the fruit had damaged him was academic. That they had saved our bacon was a certainty. I stripped one of the green fingers from a hand and kept it as a souvenir until we reached Okura's house.

Okura's house crouched in a narrow street called Mbuya Close which was on Bugalobi, one of Kampala's hills. To the front was a large garden, grassed, while at the back our friend the banana grew in profusion. For Okura, however, the fruit harvest was a sideline. He was a civil servant - a schoolteacher. I don't know what I had expected - a mud hut perhaps, beehive-shaped, but here was a modern house on the edge of a shamba with electricity, running water and bars on every window.

"Kondos," Okura had explained when I asked about the bars. "Bandits - robbers."

"Ah," I replied knowingly.

Now, we were sitting in the lounge, a large room to the front of the house. At one end was a table and six chairs; at the other, four wooden armchairs and a settee to match, upholstered with foam cushions. Our first call had been to one of the bungalow's three bedrooms where Snyder lay. His chest was swathed in bandages and he was unconscious.

"What's in there?" Dave asked Okura.

The black man shook his head sadly. "Dr Morani say three bullets still inside him. And two others have gone in and out again."

"Will the doctor be back?"

"At ten o' clock this morning."

I felt Jim's pulse. It was very weak. I wondered where bullets numbers two and three were. I knew where the first one was. A trickle of blood, bright red in colour, oozed from his lips; it had come almost certainly from his lungs.

"He needs hospitalised," Dave whispered.

I nodded but I did not agree. Snyder was beyond what hospitals could offer him; he had undergone his last operation. I kept my counsel to myself.

A cheery soul called Christianne made us eggs and toast. Afterwards we took turns to shower in cold water - wonderfully refreshing - and then we girded our loins in floral kikois that reminded me of Bing Crosby and Bob Hope in the "Road to Zanzibar". Dave had the biggest problem coming to terms with wearing his short, green and blue skirt and then me, but Heck took to his like a duck to water - he was well used to the wearing of the kilt, was he not? It was grand, he said, to feel the old testicles swing free again, unfettered by ridiculous Y-fronts or boxer shorts or flared trousers that were loose at the foot but not at the bottom!

It was a long day - the first of many that we were to be confined to Okura's bungalow. At 11 o' clock the doctor arrived. He was a Goan and one of the few Asians left in the country. Many Indian professionals had been exempted by President Amin when he had decreed, in 1972, that 90,000 Asians should quit Uganda. In the years that followed, most of the exempted ones followed their expelled compatriots, but Dr Movani had stayed. He had been born in Uganda, had married a Bugandan wife, had Ugandan children and so he had stayed. I wondered if Mrs Movani was perhaps Okura's brother-in-law's sister-in-law.

Before going in to see Snyder, the Asian doctor courteously conferred with my good self after learning that I too was a healer. He confirmed my worst fears. Snyder had indeed been hit five times. Two bullets had passed clean through his body but three were still inside him: one had lodged perilously close to his stomach; a second was lurking in the vicinity of his spinal cord, somewhere between his eighth and ninth vertebrae, while the third was without doubt probing the alveoli of his right lung.

He invited me to be in attendance when he went in to visit his patient. Snyder had regained consciousness, but the crimson foam that flecked his lips suggested that he would not be awake for long. I remained discreetly in the background while Movani made his examination. Then, when there was nothing further to be done, he made his farewells and continued on his rounds of other, less clandestine, patients.

As Movani moved from the sick bed, Snyder saw me. His eyes narrowed and his breath became even more laboured than it had been. "You!" he gasped. He tried to lift himself and, in his weakness, allowed a flailing arm to knock a glass of water from his bedside table. It crashed to the ground. He fell back on to his pillows as Dave and Heck rushed into the room.

"What . . ?"

"Whit . . !"

"He thinks it was me!" I told them, remembering - how could I have forgotten? - Beresford's betrayal.

Dave crouched by the side of the bed and, taking Snyder's hand, kneaded it tenderly. Heck stood by Snyder's other pillow and looked on, helpless.

"Jim," Mercouri whispered. "It's all right. Well, what I mean is . . . Mike. Mike's all right. He's OK. It wasn't him."

Snyder looked confused. His mind seemed to be turning over only very slowly. Then he accepted Mercouri's verdict and whispered, "Beresford", which made me suspect that his thinking wasn't slow after all. Dave nodded and I bobbed my head up and down in added confirmation. Heck said, "Bluidy bastard!"

"Where?" Snyder asked the question more with his eyebrows than with his lips.

"We don't know yet, Jim," Dave replied, "but we'll find him. You can rest assured of that."

"We'll get the bluidy bastard," Heck swore and I said, "Damned right!"

"How many?" Snyder asked next.

Dave shrugged and he replied reluctantly, "As far as we know, it's what you see, Jim. Just the four of us."

Snyder's eyes hooded over and his lips drew back in an agonised grimace.

"Twenty six men," he whispered. "I've killed twenty six men."

"It wisn'ae your fault, Colonel," Heck protested. "It wis that bluidy bastard, Beresford!"

Snyder was silent. I felt for him then tremendous pity. I have no doubt that he had had a successful career in the past, but his recent track record had surely pushed his account into the red. First there had been the debacle of the Seychelles where his men had had to work for no pay, and now Uganda where he had precious few men left *to* pay. He might have been reading my thoughts because, with considerable effort, he went on to say: "The money."

My heart quickened.

"Make sure that it goes to the families. You'll do that, Dave?"

"It's all arranged," the trusty Dave replied.

Snyder lapsed into unconsciousness and died an hour later. Dave Mercouri was devastated. He sat by the bed for the rest of the day and had almost to be prised from his vigil by a fine doctor who was concerned about the condition of his body, the state of his mind and his future ability to do his duty on payday.

I suppose Heck surprised me even more. He stood looking at his dead commanding officer with silent tears running down his face. His eyes, which before had reminded me of flint, were softened by the moisture and I almost felt sorry for him.

We wrapped Snyder in a sheet and buried him in the banana plantation behind the house. Dave made a short eulogy and remained at the grave for some time after the rest of us had adjourned to the house. When he came into the lounge he still looked very upset. Okura, sensitive to our grief, excused himself and went to his room after inviting us to help ourselves from a crate of Bell beers hauled in from the kitchen. Dave was not interested, but Heck and I sipped lager and brooded.

I hadn't really known Snyder all that well, but the other two had and their sadness and sense of loss stirred empathetic feelings in me and I was content to be miserable also.

I thought more about Beresford.

Reading my mind, Mercouri suddenly said, "I'm going to get him, boys. If it's the last thing I do. I'm going to get him and make him pay."

"Ah'm wi' you, Major," Heck pledged.

136

"Count me in," I said.

One for all and all for one. The three musketeers, that was us. Three weary musketeers who were ready for bed. Dave took over Snyder's room leaving Heck and me with more space in bedroom number three. I almost suggested that I take the single room and use it, if required, as a surgery, but, in the end, I decided not to. I was glad that I had resisted the temptation when, at seven o' clock the next morning, they brought in musketeer number four: Jean-Marc.

CHAPTER 14

I was about to deliver the coup de grace to the traitor. He looked like a pin cushion. Mercouri's trusty blade was already sticking from his side and not only was the hilt of Heck's skean dhu visible in front of his Adam's apple, its point protruded at the back of his neck. Then, as I raised my arm to pierce his black heart with my scalpel, I heard voices that woke me up.

"Doctor! Doctor!"

Oh, oh, I thought.

"Come quickly! It is your friend!"

Still only partly awake, I muttered angrily that Snyder was dead and it couldn't be him. However, I rolled off the bed, adjusted my kikoi and staggered through to the lounge.

Jean-Marc lay on the settee. He was the original cubic man: five and a half feet tall, broad and deep! His cropped, bullet-shaped head fed directly on to massive shoulders and his flattish face sported a tiny black moustache and a pruned van Dyke. He was bleeding from wounds in his left leg and shoulder.

139

He grinned when he saw me.

"'Allo, Mike," he said cheerfully. "Ça va?"

I assured him that my health was perfect and bent to examine him. As I did so, Dave Mercouri, also wakened by the voices, came through to investigate. The look of relief on his face when he recognised another survivor was immense. I wondered how long he would remain cheerful after he had shared a bedroom with Jean-Marc - always assuming I was able to keep the Belgian alive till bedtime. Jean-Marc was the loudest snorer in the world. I know. I listened to him all night once in a cabin in a submarine in the Seychelles!

Dr Movani had left a small quantity of medical supplies for Snyder and these I used to patch up Jean-Marc. He had a tunnel in the fleshy part of his thigh. An inch to the left and his femur would have been shattered. He had not been so lucky with his shoulder wound. The bullet had entered at an angle, ricochetted off his sternum and was lodged under his scapula - his shoulder blade - I could feel it!

As I probed - as gently as I could - his smile remained intact but the sweat pouring from his face told of his pain.

"Check that box again, will you Dave?" I

asked. "See if there's any morphine."

As I cleaned out Jean-Marc's leg, I heard Dave rummage in vain for the drug and then ask Okura if he had any pain-killers in the house. When he swore under his breath I knew that none was available - though a couple of aspirins were not going to have much analgesic effect anyway.

"Maybe Waragi help," Okura suggested.

"Who's he?" I asked and thought, God, not a bloody witchdoctor!

Our host handed me a bottle containing a clear liquid.

"Waragi," he said.

"Ugandan gin," Dave explained.

"Any good?"

"It works. Should he?"

I shrugged. Probably not. But it was all there was and I had to get a bullet out of a Belgian without barbiturates. I also knew that *I* needed a drink!

"Get two glasses," I ordered, "and some for yourselves if you feel inclined."

Dave pursed his lips, seemed about to deliver

some form of rebuke, thought better of it and disappeared into the kitchen for the glasses. He returned with two. He poured a thimbleful into one and half-filled the other with the raw spirit. I pretended to reach for the stiffer drink, stopped and grinned up at Dave. He held my eye and then, thank God, relaxed and smiled wryly. He placed the quadruple in Jean-Marc's outstretched paw and gave me my sixth of a gill.

"Iz pity iz no' Cognac," Jean-Marc said, "but . . ." He tossed half of it down his throat and made a face. "Iz beeg pity," he added. Then he finished his medicine and held the empty glass out for a refill. While I knocked back my own meagre allocation - it would have tasted OK with ice and lemon and tonic - Dave tipped the bottle once more and restocked Jean-Marc's tumbler. By the time the wounded man had downed his second half pint a glaze had come over his eyes and he looked relaxed.

It took much sweat and tears - and not all of them Jean-Marc's - to get that damned bullet out of the Belgian's shoulder. By the time I was done, he had, mercifully, passed out. I bandaged him up and accepted a second glass of Waragi - a decent measure this time - from Dave Mercouri. "Good work, doc," he said with a smile.

We made Jean-Marc as comfortable as possible on the couch and then went through to the kitchen for breakfast.

"Will he be all right?" Dave asked.

I nodded. "He's as strong as an ox. He should be OK."

"So now we are four."

"D'Artagnan has arrived," I said.

"Huh?"

"The fourth musketeer."

"Oh yeah."

We were joined by Heck and Okura and had toast and coffee standing up.

"Two missions; two failures. Your record as a soldier ain't good, Mike," Dave said.

"You're a jinx, Mike," Heck added.

I was pleased. It was the first time that the little Glaswegian had ever acknowledged me, let alone called me by my first name. I coughed. "This mission is not over yet," I declared, hoping that nobody could see that my tongue was wedged firmly in my cheek. "There are four of us left; we could still get him."

Dave shook his head and I relaxed.

"Not a chance. Not even if we still had our full complement. Amin's been warned. He'll be guarded tighter than a fish's asshole for the next six months."

"So that's it," I muttered, pleased.

"We've still got to get back," Dave reminded me gently.

"Whit d'ye think, major?" Heck asked. "How're we goanie dae it?"

Dave turned to our host. "Mr Okura," he said, "do you have any suggestions?"

Okura nodded. "It is simple," he replied. "You must wait here until the curfew is lifted. Then we smuggle you across the border into Kenya, or Tanzania, or Zaire. It is for you to choose."

Dave thought for a moment. "Zaire is in the right direction," he replied, "but Kenya would probably be our best bet. There are more white faces there and everybody speaks English. Although," he added with a grin, "that might not be much of an advantage to Heck."

"Eh? Whit d'ye mean?" the Glaswegian demanded.

"How long do you think before they call off the curfew?" Dave asked.

The Ugandan shrugged. "A few days, a few weeks. Who knows what the madman will decide? Perhaps in a few days it will be lifted during daylight hours. I hope that you will grow to like matoke. Supplies of other commodities are scarce and besides, it would not be safe to purchase many items: the men of the PSU are everywhere."

I made a face, but then remembered how the good old banana had probably saved our lives.

Later that day Jean-Marc regained consciousness.

"Comment ça va, mon brave?"

When had Maurice Chevalier come in?

Dave did a double take.

I did a double double take.

Guess who?

None other.

Heck!

For the next three minutes Mercouri, Okura, Christianne and I were treated to a dialogue that might not have been *justement* at a *soirée* in the Academie Française but would not have been too *de trops* on a sandy balustrade of Fort Beau Geste. Of course there was an excuse for Jean-Marc, but the 'r's rolling from Heck's battle-scarred lips would have warmed the cockles of old Charles de Gaulle's heart.

Of course Dave joined in - he *would* be fluent in French, wouldn't he? As for me, I listened carefully, caught the odd word or two and chipped in with a "oui" or a "d'accord" when I thought they might be appropriate. Only our host and his house-girl had no French; they slipped from the room and left us to it.

Later, in English, I said to my countryman, "I didn't know". He shrugged - Gallic to the end - and replied in something akin to the mother tongue: "Ye didn'ae ask, did ye?" He was, of course, right.

I examined Jean-Marc and was happy to announce that he would live. He wasn't going to be able to travel for some time but then, we weren't going anywhere in the short term and so it didn't matter. His reaction to the identity of the traitor was predictable.   "Bâtard! I weel keel him!"

"Ye'll huv tae stand in line, mate," Heck warned him.

We stayed with Okura for three weeks. After

only three days the curfew was lifted from dawn till dusk and normal work resumed for most. Okura returned to school and we were left at home. The only time we went out to take the air was at night and even then we strayed no further than the banana patch behind the house.

I slipped into our sedentary routine quite easily, as did Jean-Marc. Heck busied himself creating masterpieces from very little in the kitchen although I think that part of the attraction there was Christianne. Dave alone took the inactivity hard. He paced the house, muttering constantly to himself and really making quite a nuisance of himself.

We passed the time reading and listening to music. Okura had a reel to reel Akai tape recorder and just about every recording Frank Sinatra ever made. We also listened to Radio Uganda which confirmed daily that President Amin was alive and kicking; the BBC World Service kept us up to date on the international scene. We all got to like matoke and ate lots of fruit that kept us healthy.

CHAPTER 15

We heard nothing of Beresford until our second Sunday at Bugalobi. Okura, who had been to church, returned home looking very excited. "Your friend," he told us, "the one you wish to meet again."

"Beresford?" Dave snapped. He was doing press-ups on the woven mat that covered most of the living room floor. He got up and glowered at our host. Okura sat down.

"My cousin," he began (it *had* to be a relative) "has just returned from Tororo - on the Kenyan border. He was having a drink with a man from the customs service who told him that a white man passed through the border on Wednesday. He was accompanied by an officer in the Ugandan army. He did not have to open his baggage. He was as tall as I and had fair hair and blue eyes. He was called 'Christopher'."

"Beresford!"

Dave spat out the word. Heck and I gathered round and Jean-Marc looked up from his book. We tried to bully more information from Okura, but there was no more. What was clear, however, was the direction our escape route would now take. What was not clear was just where in Kenya Beresford had gone. That he had not flown from Entebbe to Nairobi suggested that his destination was short of the Kenyan capital. Perhaps he fancied a safari before he went back to England with his thirty pieces of silver.

"Where could he have gone?" Dave asked Okura.

The Ugandan thought for a moment and then he said with a shrug, "Kenya is a very large country . . . .

"Do you have a map?"

"Yes. I shall get it."

He returned with a school atlas already opened at the page devoted to East Africa. He pointed with a broad forefinger. "There, Tororo. There, Nairobi. Perhaps he goes to Nakuru; perhaps to Nanyuki. Perhaps he wishes to climb Mount Kenya."

"OK. First things first. How do we get across the border?" Dave asked.

The Ugandan thought for a moment. "You must be patient," he said. "Something will be arranged."

I am sure that Okura was pleased to see the back of us. He certainly looked relieved when Mawembe's ambulance, with us inside, trundled down Mbuya Close and headed east. Mawembe himself was up front with the driver. He had done well, had used his initiative to help us on our way.

Apparently part of the roof at the cement factory at Tororo had collapsed - not an uncommon occurrence! There were many casualties. When Mawembe had heard that help was to be sent from Kampala, he had managed to arrange passage for us to the border in the ambulance which would then collect injured survivors and bring them back to hospital in the capital. Okura and his friends produced for us clothes and footwear that were adequate, if not Savile Row. We all wore flared trousers but only mine were a good fit. The bottoms of Dave's flapped half way up his shins while those of Heck and Jean-Marc had to be folded - in Heck's case three times - so that they would not trail on the ground. I was also lucky with the shirt - blue cotton, that fitted me like a glove. Dave's was white and Jean-Marc's green but neither garment covered its new owner's belly-button. Heck sat in the back of the ambulance and looked as if he was drowning in a lavender top that would have fitted the other two if they had not refused point blank to wear it. Our flip-flops were blue.

The journey to Tororo was uneventful.

Through the back windows we saw the hills of Kampala retreat and then disappear. The road was now flanked by fields of coffee and sugar estates and, later, terraced hills that bristled with tea bushes. In the distance we saw the odd group of huts made from mud and wattle that reminded me of Robinson Crusoe's hat. I had thought that houses like these were only seen in Bob Hope movies, but I was wrong. Wisps of smoke from nearby campfires declared the homes occupied. The only animals we saw of the four legged variety were dogs - and mangy curs they were too. Where was all the game? The antelopes and the elephant? The zebra and the buffalo?

"They've eaten them all," Dave said when I spoke my thoughts out loud.

The ambulance stopped on a hill overlooking Tororo. Heck, Jean-Marc and I waved goodbye to Mawembe and his driver and stepped aside to allow Dave to say it properly. We were going to have to stay under cover for only an hour or so before darkness swallowed up our passage to Kenya.

"See that big building down there," Dave said as we looked down on the town. "That's the Rock. The last watering hole in Uganda."

"You've been there," I said. He nodded.

Although the hotel seemed deserted, I was sure that the bar would be open. I wanted to suggest a visit, but I realized that it was out of the question. Even I knew that there were now only about seventeen white men left in Uganda and that if four of them suddenly descended upon the snug at the Rock Hotel then the PSU would know about it before we could finish our first pint and/or pernod and water; our goose would be cooked and we would be flung once again into the dungeon at Makindye.

"Several times," Dave replied. "How d'you fancy moseyin' on down there for a quickie?"

"You mean a drink?" I said disapprovingly.

"Why not?"

I hesitated.

"Well", I muttered. "There can't be many white men around who haven't been involved in a recent counter-coup attempt. Don't you think we would sort of stand out?"

"Oh, *we* would, he laughed, "but *you*, in your sartorial elegance, wouldn't - and you could always say that you were a doctor on your way to the cement factory."

"And that I've just dropped in for four or five

pints before I start to operate?"

He smiled. "Now, now, doctor. You're being obtuse again. I thought you would jump at the chance."

"You're right, Dave. I normally would. It's just that . . . why *would* I drop into the hotel - and why do you want me to?"

"I want you to buy some whisky - half a dozen bottles if you can."

"Whisky? Why?"

"We need them for services still to be rendered. You can say that you're short of pain killers and that the whisky will be a good substitute."

"What if there are soldiers - or the PSU?"

"Case the joint first. Any sign of trouble, you abort. Use your charm, doctor - and have a drink while you're there."

Heck and Jean-Marc grinned their encouragement and so there was nothing else for it: I *had* to go to the pub for a drink! Dave gave me some American dollars and patted me on the arm. Somehow I felt like the sacrificial lamb.

I kept to the bushes that fringed the hotel car park and took the path that led to reception. Self-consciously I entered the hotel. I found myself in a large lobby littered with wickerwork tables and chairs but devoid of people. A long reception desk was unmanned, but beside it there was a sign that said "bar". I peeked in the open door. As Dave Mercouri would have put it, the joint sure wasn't jumpin'. I went in and strolled, more confidently now, up to the bar. As I leaned on the counter and strained to read the labels on the bottles that lined the shelves I began to salivate - and not just because of the bottles of Scotch and gin and vodka in front of me. A beautiful pair of bulging buttocks beckoned from below the gantry and begged to be fondled. They were firm and yet soft-looking. They were trying to wriggle out of thin, pale green cotton through which waist and slanting leg elastic peaked in erotic relief. I felt a stirring deep inside that had been absent since the night at the Coconut Grove but, although sorely tempted, I did not touch.

I cleared my throat. The figure straightened and the outlines of her knickers disappeared in the looseness of her dress. She turned to me and smiled. She was lovely - and a whole lot of woman.

"Jambo, bwana."

I felt like Bob Hope.

"I'd like a White Cap, please - and have a drink yourself."

Her plump cheeks wobbled and a dazzling smile lit up her face. She chose a half litre bottle from a cold tray and carefully poured the beer. She handed me the glass and smiled again. My heart somersaulted with lust.

"And you?" I prompted, pointing at her and raising my eyebrows. She bent again and produced a bottle of bitter lemon which she opened, poured and sipped. Her eyes never left my face and mine left hers only to assess and then to feast on her lovely bosom.

"I need whisky," I said. She smiled even more broadly and took another drink. She obviously had as much English as I had Swahili. However, we had sign language and I had American dollars and money talks and sometimes it is misunderstood. As I took out my wad of notes her eyes sparkled and, before I could tell her in mime that I wanted Scotch, she took a ten from the top of the pile and then she took my hand. She gripped my middle finger and walked the length of the bar to a hatch through which she drew me gently. With her free hand she opened a door behind her and pulled me into the darkness.

She let my finger go, but she was still close to me - I could smell her musk. I waited with growing excitement. Then she turned on the light. She was stark naked. She sat on a table and her arms and legs were outstretched and beckoning. I allowed them to take me. In seconds my flares were around my ankles. I cupped her bottom and I lifted her on to me. She locked her legs behind my back and took some of her weight on her hands. I thought I had just strapped on a bucking bronco. She screamed in ecstasy and I knew that she was faking but it didn't matter. I wasn't and she was trying to please. She succeeded. Later, in the bar, I managed to convey to her that the rest of my cash was for whisky. For $90 she gave me four bottles of Johnny Walker Red Label and a plastic carrier bag. I finished my drink, waved her goodbye and retraced my steps to where the boys waited among the banana trees.

"That was quick," Dave said. He was right. I'd been away only twenty minutes.

"Any trouble?"

I shook my head. "I managed four bottles, OK?"

"Four? Good. That should do it. Well done. You have one yourself?"

I nodded. A quickie, I thought.

"Anybody give you funny looks?"

"There was nobody there - except the barmaid."

"Pretty?"

"She was OK."

"Just OK, huh? Just as well, I suppose. "The Rock has a terrible reputation - or it had, at any rate."

"What do you mean?"

"The girls there. Semi-pros and not too healthy in the venereal department."

Shit! I should have known! And here I was surrounded by banana trees and not a shot of penicillin in sight.

Heck had a question. "Major, ye're no' thinkin' o' bribin' yer way through customs, are ye?"

Mercouri turned to me with an eyebrow cocked. I translated.

"Yes and no," he replied. "This is the plan. We wait till it's dark and then we go into town. We find Bokassa Avenue. Number 42. We ask for Sam. The whisky is for him. He's going to guide us across the border."

Dave explained that Mawembe had told him about the arrangements when he had said goodbye.

"Don't tell me," I interrupted, "Sam is

Mawembe's brother-in-law, right?"

Dave looked at me oddly. "How did you know?" he asked.

I shrugged.

"Anyway, Sam apparently knows the back roads into Kenya. He does a little exporting-importing in his spare time."

"And the rest of the time?"

"He's a custom's officer."

OK.

Darkness fell quickly. It was 6.45. The sky, suddenly black, was studded with stars that seemed huge and unnaturally close. A half moon smiled down on us and gave us sufficient light to see where we were going.

Dave seemed to know the way and soon found Bokassa Avenue which was off Idi-Amin Parade. Number 42 was next door to number 26. Never mind. He knocked gently on the door of a small, whitewashed house. After a minute or two it opened a fraction. Dave whispered the Swahili equivalent of "open sesame" and we were invited inside.

The present of four bottles of Scotch made

our guide very happy. In return his wife presented us with steaming bowls of matoke and he, Sam, led us across the border later that night. He did not offer us a dram.

It was all so easy. The border separating Uganda and Kenya had immigration and customs posts - single storeyed shacks - for each country. In between was a stretch of about two hundred yards - "no-man's land". We followed Sam, Indian file, on a course parallel to and not a hundred yards from the road. We heard voices and laughter coming from the guards, but they neither heard nor saw us. At nine o' clock that evening Sam bade us "Kwaheri" and disappeared back into the bush. We were alone in Kenya.

CHAPTER 16

"If," Dave had pronounced while he stared at Okura's atlas, "he hasn't headed for Nairobi - and I agree that if he had wanted to go there he would probably have flown - then he's either gone south to Kusumi (unlikely), stopped off at Eldoret or Nakuru - or even Naivasha - or, and this is my bet: he's gone to the Mount Kenya Safari Club - or Tree-tops."

I had nodded wisely. If Mercouri thought that Beresford had done a Tarzan and was now swinging from creepers in the jungle somewhere in Kenya then who was I to contradict him? Let some other mug do it. Heck was apparently thinking some way along the same lines as myself, but he blew it. He opened his big mouth and put his foot in it. "Christ," he muttered, "ah kent the bastard wis a swine but ah didn'ae peg'm for a bloody baboon."

"Treetops," Dave explained patiently, "is one of the most famous safari lodges in East Africa. It is situated in the White Highlands near Nyeri, not far from Mount Kenya. There." He pointed to the map. I nodded again, said, "Yes" and treated Heck to a withering look that I made sure he saw.

"But first, from where we are," Dave continued, "we hit Nanyuki and the Mount Kenya Safari Club. There."

"OK," the Glaswegian conceded. "But even if he went there, will he still *be* there? It's been three weeks."

Dave shrugged. "Only one way to find out. If he *has* been there maybe he's left a forwarding address. If not, we continue to Nairobi and make enquiries there."

So that was the plan. Very simple. Go to Mount Kenya, find Beresford and see that he got what was coming to him. The only problem was that it was half past nine on a dark night and we were on a deserted road half a mile from the border of a country run by a maniac whom we had just failed to overthrow and who was not renowned for forgiving the trespasses of those who sinned against him! And talking of trespassing, we were in Kenya illegally. Dave and I were the only ones with passports - unstamped; Jean-Marc and Heck of course had travelled to Uganda without papers. We looked like something the cat had left outside - except me, of course - as we trudged down the road in the dark with only a couple of hundred of miles to walk - in flip-flops!

****

"We need wheels," Dave said for the umpteenth time.

We had been walking for an hour and had yet to see a car that we could hijack. We had a plan ready. As soon as we saw the lights of an approaching vehicle Dave, Heck and I would hide in the ditch by the side of the road while Jean-Marc would lie on the tarmac. When the car stopped we would jump out, requisition it and continue our journey in comfort. Of course, Jean-Marc was not too happy to be cast as road block, but he was the obvious choice - he was by far the most likely to be spotted by an on-coming driver who would think twice about trying to drive over an obstacle of our Belgian's bulk. However, he knew that he had no chance if it went to a vote and so, with less than his usual good grace, he agreed to play the roadblock.

"There's somethin' comin'!"

Heck heard it first and whispered the warning. In no time flat we were in our positions. The vehicle was approaching fast from the east and I remember thinking with surprise: who in their right minds wants to go *into* Uganda? We saw the headlight beams before the lamps themselves appeared on the road: a pair of staring eyes that floated in the darkness. Spreadeagled in the middle of the road, Jean-Marc looked, for the first time in his life, insignificant.

The car almost failed to stop. It was only about twenty yards short of mounting Jean-Marc when the driver presumably saw the danger. He must have wrenched the wheel at the same time as he stood on the brakes. Rubber screeching on metal and rubber on tarmac pierced the night and the car, a big black Mercedes, slewed and skidded sideways the last few yards. It stopped inches short of Jean-Marc.

Dave and Heck, who were screaming like Dervishes, reached it just ahead of me. They wrenched open the driver's door and the rear door and launched themselves inside the vehicle. As I mounted guard outside, I heard them go to work. Sounds of force being applied were followed by yells of pain and anger. Jean-Marc rose from his side of the Mercedes, opened the other rear door and piled in too. The car rocked dangerously and I thought it was going to overturn. The noise was horrendous, the grunts feral, the yelling crazed.

Suddenly a body shot out of the back of the car. Before I could get out of the way it enveloped me in an octopus embrace and I staggered backwards, tripped and fell heavily into the ditch by the side of the road. An armpit encased in cloth was a suction cup over my face. I couldn't breathe. In panic, I twisted my body to escape suffocation and almost wished I hadn't bothered. What a dreadful smell! Whoever was pinning me to the ground hadn't washed for weeks! But it was his b.o. that galvanised me into action. I surged upwards and flailed out at him with both arms. I howled in agony as the knuckles of my right hand bounced off his skull. Then he lay still and I was on top of him. I held my breath, rolled off his body and stood up. My knuckles were sore - at best they were badly bruised. He did not move.

As I massaged my hand I became aware that there were no noises coming from the car. All I could hear were the clicking of the cicada and the rasp of my own breathing. I climbed back out of the ditch. The Merc straddled the road. Its headlights, still burning brightly, picked out rows of tea bushes and a solitary acacia tree that looked like a gallows. A torso, head down, sprawled half in, half out of the driver's door.

Who - ?

The Mercedes reminded me of the Marie Celeste: apart from Thomas Torso who turned out to be Black Thomas Torso, the car looked empty. I looked inside. Dave Mercouri was sprawled, face down, across the long front seat. He was breathing heavily. He seemed to have four legs, two of which were knees up and black. In the back Heck and Jean-Marc sat low. Jean-Marc was stroking his beard with an enormous paw and Heck was picking his nose.

"What's up, doc?" the little Glaswegian said. "See what we've got here," he added with a grin. I peered into the back of the car - sardine tin more like - and there, under my two friends' feet, was a pair of crumpled figures.

With a grunt, Dave back-heeled Thomas Torso fully from the car and wriggled, feet first, out of the front seat. He then carelessly hauled the unconscious figure on which he had lain out on to the road. The two in the back did likewise with their victims. They were all Africans, young, smartly dressed and liable to be hors de combat for some considerable time. Except for the octopus who had jumped me - correction, who had landed on me: *his* tongue protruded horribly from generous lips and he was extremely dead. Around his neck I could see the twisted ends of Heck's garrotte. Poor fellow.

Poor fellows.

Poor fellows nothing!

A search of the car and its erstwhile owners revealed three hand guns - fortunately for us, well stashed in trousers pockets - four knives, wallets bulging with dollars and Sterling and Kenyan and Ugandan shillings and identity papers signed by Idi Amin himself. And five pairs of reflecting sunglasses. We had captured a covey of PSU tearaways returning, perhaps, from a visit to the fleshpots of Kenya. I examined their faces closely and was disappointed not to recognise any of my assailants of the Coconut Grove.

We took the cash, the knives and the pistols and smashed the sunglasses with our heels at the side of the tarmac. We also relieved the men of what clothes fitted better than our own and bundled the youths, still out for the count, into the short, thick grass where the one with the wire collar lay. Dave and I were lucky with shoes. Heck retrieved the garrotte, cleaned it and tucked it away for a rainy day. Then we boarded the Merc and, with Heck driving, headed for the Aberdares and Mount Kenya.

We stopped at a single open dukah on the outskirts of Eldoret and bought fruit and bread and a bottle of whisky - on my suggestion - for medicinal purposes. There were a few hotels in the town's main street, but we decided not to delay; we wanted to be as far away as possible by the time the sleeping beauties behind us woke up.

We left the main Nairobi road just before Nakuru and were climbing out of the Rift valley before I even realised we had descended into it. We by-passed Thomson's Falls without seeing them and reached the gates of the Game Park in which the Mount Kenya Safari Club and Game Ranch was situated. They were locked and had been so since nightfall.

"Some hotel this is," I complained. "Can't get in after dark - can't even see the damn place."

"Thae padlocks look easy, major. D'ye want me tae . . . ."

Dave shook his head. "No, Heck. Until we can change cars we do nothing that might attract attention. If we got through the gates and reached the Club we would be doing just that - you don't arrive at these lodges after dark; you come for lunch - then you can stay for dinner and the night."

"So what do we do, then?" I asked.

"We spend the night in the car. Tomorrow we see if there's any room at the inn."

"An' we see if that bastard's thair - or been thair!"

"Aye."

Dave told Heck to drive on for a couple of miles. "There," he pointed. "Off the road."

Heck directed the car as he was bid and drew up beside a clump of bushes. He switched off the engine.

"Sun up is at about seven," Dave told us, "but I want us to be on our way at six."

"Six. Why six?" I asked.

"Because, gentlemen, by the crack of dawn tomorrow - today - we shall be on safari." He bade us goodnight and within seconds he was asleep. (So that was his secret! The Jean-Marc volcano never stood a chance!)

It got cold. Well, what do you expect eleven thousand feet up? Kampala is only 4000 feet above sea level and balmy in the evening, but up in the Aberdares at night it's chilly. At Mount Kenya, 17000 feet up, there's snow all the year round for goodness sake! We hadn't felt any discomfort while the engine had been running, but now we did. Then, at my suggestion, Heck investigated the boot and there found our luck: five jackets of varying sizes and two hold-alls crammed with sweaters and dirty underwear.

I slept only fitfully; fortunately for the rest of us, Jean-Marc did not sleep at all. For long stretches I stared out of the window at the bushes - they and my reflection were all that I could see - and thought about my life. In Newcastle as a boy; at Durham University; as a young doctor in the Midlands. I remembered with distaste my wife, Joan, a doctor too, who had inherited her father's practice and had become, briefly, my boss. I thought fondly for the main part of the Seychelles where I had first become a soldier of fortune and where I had found and lost the lovely Sue Dailly. The memory of the Lady in Blue at the Cardinal Club made me shut my eyes and seek sleep.

It was then that I became more aware of the noises. The sounds of Africa. The incessant zinging of countless insects and, as dawn approached, the singing of the birds and the screeching of playful primates and the roar of some carnivore frustrated, perhaps, by the escape of her intended breakfast-victim.

But the most dangerous animals around were the three men beside me that I called friends. Their presence gave me much comfort; I felt safe with them, even in the middle of Africa.

Dave Mercouri, policeman, soldier, now soldier-of fortune. A born leader with a moral streak that hopefully would not rub off on me. Dependable Dave, our Treasurer.

Jean-Marc. A tower of strength with no past - or one that he would talk about - before his time as a Foreign Legionnaire that preceded his stint in the Congo. A quiet man, a gentle man. A man who was as undemanding of your time as he was of your emotions. He had been with Snyder the longest, but if he missed our late leader, he no longer showed it.

Then there was Heck. I think that he was

called that because 'heck' was the only expletive that he did not use - though I had noticed that he was careful with his cussing in front of Mercouri and used words no stronger than "bloody" or "shite" or "bastard" when the major was present. Brought up in post-war Glasgow, Heck had stayed on in the army after completing his National Service. He had served in Cyprus, Germany and Northern Ireland. The army had taught him to cook and then, somewhere along the line, had kicked him out for misdemeanors and/or crimes unspecified. Heck had gone back to Glasgow, got drunk one night with some mates and woke up the next morning on a French train bound for Paris. In his pocket was the address of the recruitment office of the Foreign Legion. He had joined up, spent three years in Algiers, met Jean-Marc and learnt French.

At six thirty Dave woke up. He stretched, wandered outside to relieve himself and then had an apple.

"Ready for a new experience?" he asked. "I suggest you take a leak first."

When we were all back in the car, Heck started her up and we returned to the Park gate. A sleepy looking ranger sold us tickets and then we were inside the overgrown zoo.

Overgrown zoo!

What an idiot!

If you've never been on a safari in somewhere like Kenya, you haven't lived. The next five hours, couped up in the front seat of a sticky and increasingly hot motor car were the most magical I have ever experienced outside a nymphomaniac's bedroom. The sounds of foraging animals were everywhere and, even before the sun rose to light the grasslands in pinks and oranges and purples, we saw game - shadows still but moving ones of predator and prey going about the business of staying alive. We travelled the game park tracks - indeed it is strictly forbidden to deviate from them. These meandered through the savannah and snaked under trees full of monkeys with colour in their antics and birds with astonishing variety in their colour. They snaked past the haunts of rhinoceros and skirted the swamps where hippos wallowed and blew and looked enormous and deceptively docile. But mostly they twisted through the grass and the shrubbery where the antelopes roamed: the gazelle and the wildebeeste, the hartebeeste and the kudo, the impala and the others.

"Look at that wee buffalo!" Heck's shriek made me jump.

Dave laughed. "That's not a buffalo," he said. "It's a warthog boar. See. His tail!"

172

As he spoke, the little animal, aware at last of intruders, squealed. Its tail stiffened, straightened and pointed skywards like the aerial on a TV-detector van. It screeched again and, from longer grass nearby, half a dozen tiny bodies, with their tails also in the air, scurried after their fleeing parent and disappeared into the undergrowth.

"They're like the dodgems at the fair!" Heck cried.

"Buffalo!" I scoffed.

The car was full of good humour.

"Look at that! " I cried, my eyes again to the road in front.

"Where?"

"What ?

"Oh!"

"Oh!"

Thirty yards ahead and blocking our way was the biggest animal I have ever seen.

"An elephant!"

"A big elephant!"

"Look at his trunk!

"Look at his tusks!"

"Look at - look out! He's coming this way!"

And so he was. A fifteen feet tall and God knows how many tons weight of pacy pachyderm with enormous rheumy eyes and tilting tusks seemed determined to teach us that we were driving the wrong way up a one-way elephant walk! Heck hastily engaged reverse gear, but before he could back off the track, the elephant stopped. He stepped off the road, gave us a last baleful look and ambled off.

"Whew! That was a close one!"

"Big bloody shite!"

The rest of the morning flew by. At one o' clock, we reluctantly left the safari trails and followed the signs for the Safari Club and 'civilisation'. We parked the car well away from the front door of a magnificent building with large windows and larger verandas that overlooked a wide pool of water.

"See that?" Dave pointed to the pool. "See down there? That's a waterhole. Before sunrise and at dusk those verandas will be full of people armed with binoculars and cameras. To see the game. That's when the beasts come to drink." When we all made to get out of the car Dave cautioned, "Only two, only two to go in."

I nodded. Only two. The two most respectable. Must be Dave and me.

"You and me, Mike."

Just so.

The two most respectable.

Heck and Jean-Marc didn't seem to mind.

Dave and I entered reception and enquired about vacancies. While the clerk checked his lists, Dave commandeered the Register. He spun it round without asking permission and glanced at the open page. He flipped back a page.

The second entry from the top of this page was for one 'Christopher Beresford'. He had left the Safari Club on the 7th of September. Exactly two weeks before.

CHAPTER 17

Dave pushed the register back to the clerk and treated the man to a huge grin   "A friend of ours," he explained. "Looks like we just missed him."

The clerk waited politely.

"Mr Beresford," Dave went on. It was like pulling teeth. "Yeah. D'you remember him? A Brit - he was here two weeks ago. Tall, fair. He didn't say where he was headed, did he?" Dave fanned himself with a ten dollar bill.   The clerk accepted the banknote, pocketed it and found his tongue. "Sorry for that, suh. Mr Beresford not leave forwading address I think. But I check." He consulted a ledger pulled out from below his counter. The book of forwarding addresses. Beresford's was not there. The clerk apologised again and moved away before Dave could ask for a refund.

We moved off too. We did not want to be remembered as the 'persistent nosey pair'. We walked in silence until we reached one of the open verandas that overlooked the water-hole; both were unattended.

"Maybe we should rest up here for a day or two," I suggested. "We could keep our ears open and maybe learn something about Beresford's movements. And I wouldn't mind getting to see some lions."

Dave smiled and I thought he would agree, but then he shook his head and I knew that lion were not on the menu.

"Safari-in's got to you, huh?" he remarked. "Well, the lion'll have to wait, Mike. Anyway, we rested long enough in Kampala. We got to get crackin'. The sooner we get to Nairobi and make a deal with a second hand car dealer I happen to know, the happier I'll be. They say that the arm of Idi Amin is as long as his memory."

So that was that. We were Nairobi bound. Of course Beresford could have taken a toddle up Mount Kenya, but eventually, if he had not already done so, he would surely have to go to the capital.

"He'll have money," Dave pointed out. "And in Nairobi there are not all that many places to go to when you got plenny bananas. We'll find him."

There was no point arguing. I would much rather have spent a few days on safari, but I had no bananas - Dave held what cash we had in Kenya and he was the one with access to the money that was coming to us for not killing Idi Amin. And so where he went I was sure to follow, even though my resolve to bring Beresford to book had weakened.

"How about lunch?" I suggested.

"Not here. We'll stop somewhere with lower profile."

We returned to the car and told the boys what we had learnt.

"So we better get goin' then," Heck declared. His thirst for justice or vengeance was no less than before.

On our way south there was a line drawn on the road separating the northern hemisphere from the southern and a sign that confirmed that here indeed was the equator. I was disappointed. I hadn't expected a band to play us across but stories of "crossing the line", remembered from my youth, made me associate the crossing with a party. But, then, we were on no cruise ship and this was no cruise. Soon after, we passed Mount Kenya. Kenya's highest mountain, Africa's second tallest after Kilimanjaro, was, as ever, snow-capped. We stopped for a bite to eat at Thika and then drove through to Nairobi.

Nairobi was a city of contrasts. My first impression was one of poverty and squalor. The outlying suburbs were shanty towns of tin and cardboard and corrugated iron which housed - and I use the word loosely - thousands of people who left the land because they believed that the streets of the city were paved with gold. Other suburbs were parklands with enormous villas lost in acres of gardens, full of colour, manicured. The city centre bristled with skyscrapers and tree-lined avenues - and the Leaning Tower of Pisa, for God's sake, in the guise of the Nairobi Hilton!

Dave dropped us at the New Stanley Hotel and said that he would meet us at its Thorn Tree restaurant as soon as he could do a deal on the car. We sat alfresco and tucked into hamburgers and chips as the whole of Nairobi passed by. Chris Beresford did not pass by so maybe he wasn't in the capital.

Dave was gone over two hours. When he returned he was smiling.

"Got rid of it then?" I asked.

He nodded. "We are now the proud owners of a Fiat 128. My friend, Abdullah, couldn't believe his luck. A Mercedes SL480 for a Fiat 128 - plus registration document. I think we all did fairly well, don't you?"

Heck summed up the deal neatly. "Aye," he

said, "considerin' that yesterday we didn'ae huv a car at a', we're no' doin' too badly!"

Dave called for service and ordered food which we watched him eat over cups of coffee.

"I've booked us in here," he told us, "for one night at least. And, by the way, these hotels don't come cheap but don't worry. Guess who's footing the bill?"

"Idi Amin?"

"Bonnie Prince Cherlie?"

"Christopher Beresford?"

"Correct, Jean-Marc. The dough will come from his account."

"So he has no access?"

Dave shook his head. "Let me finish this," he said, "and then we'll go upstairs and I'll fill you in on the financial details - and how we're going to track Beresford down. And, we'll crack that bottle of Scotch if Mike didn't finish it in the car!"

I protested that there was still plenty left, but suggested that we pick up a few cold beers for our summit meeting.

Room 642 at the New Stanley Hotel had a

181

high panoramic view over the city. We looked down Kenyatta Avenue to Uhuru Highway. Uhuru. Freedom. Too much of which commodity we all believed Beresford had enjoyed already.

"Abdullah has contacts everywhere," Dave told us. "If Beresford is in Nairobi, he'll know by tonight. If he's been and gone, he'll know that by tonight as well. If he's never been here, Abdullah will be sure of that tomorrow."

Good. That was Beresford out of the way. Now. What about the cash? I didn't think it good manners to ask, but I figured Heck wouldn't stand on ceremony - he'd just come right out with it. He didn't have to.

"Right," Dave said. He stood with his back to the window and was clutching a tumbler full of Scotch. "As you know, everybody was promised an advance, payable regardless of the outcome of the mission. The rest of the money was up front too but, naturally, with strings attached. This is the way it was to work. The loot was deposited in two bank accounts in Zurich. The first - and smaller - contained the deposits. These would be payable when we set foot on Ugandan soil. Two people were authorised to dispense this money: Snyder and me."

Watch you don't hurt yourself, Dave, I thought.

And come away from that window!

"But don't worry if I get bumped off," he continued. "Because, naturally, in a caper like this, it was always on the cards that Snyder and I might buy it. So, we have left instructions that your shares be paid on demand - to you or to your estates - unless, for some reason, your allocation is frozen."

"Frozen! And who can authorise that?" I asked.

"Guess who?" Dave smiled. "And I already have. Frozen a share. Guess whose?"

We all grinned now. Beresford may have been paid off in Uganda but at least he was to receive no further payment for his treachery; he would, however, ensure that *our* stay in Kenya was comfortable.

"Unfortunately," Dave went on, "we'll have to pass on the second instalment - the really big money. It 's in the other account and was to be made available only if our mission was successful."

Which it hadn't been. Because of Beresford. I wondered if we would have succeeded if Beresford had been straight. Correction. If *they* would have succeeded. I had been tucked away in my little domino dungeon, hadn't I? I would probably have been bludgeoned to death when it had been my turn and would now either be pushing up the daisies in the cemetery outside the prison or else causing some crocodile acute indigestion somewhere in the River Nile. Looking at it like that, I really had Beresford to thank for being alive. Thanks, Chris. Good old Chris. Good old -

"Mike! Mike?"

"Eh? What?"

"You still with us, doc?"

"Yes. Oh yes - I was just thinking."

"Meditating, more like."

"I was thinking about Beresford. He sure has a lot to answer for."

"He sure does, Mike. But don't worry. He's coming to the end of the line. We're closing in."

Word came through from Abdullah while we were in the hotel restaurant having dinner. When he returned from the telephone, Dave's face was lit up like I had never seen it before and it proclaimed excitement, anticipation and a look of cruelty all at once. I knew before he told us that Beresford was in town.

"He's here. At the Hilton. Room 369. Let's

go."

Heck and Jean-Marc were on their feet somewhere between the "6" and the "9". I looked at the pink flesh of my Tournedos Rossini, sighed and followed the merry men from the restaurant. I had to run to keep up.

The night was balmy, but I was glad that Dave had bought us - or had it been Beresford's treat? - new clothes that included a jacket for wearing at night. Nairobi is six thousand feet up, remember. The Thorn Tree was quieter than it had been in the afternoon. So were the streets. Although the Hilton Hotel was only a couple of blocks from the New Stanley we took the car. Dave took the wheel himself and told us what Abdullah had just relayed to him.

"He's been in Nairobi most of the last two weeks - apart from a few days in the Masai Mara. It seems he's as keen on safari as you are, Mike."

I didn't like the association but I said nothing.

"He arrived with a Ugandan who has since gone home. So now he's on his own - apart from a succession of lady friends who have latched on to him. He's been spending money like there's no tomorrow."

Dave stopped speaking and we were all

aware of the poignancy and the, hopefully, prophetic nature of his last remarks. We parked in the official car park where Dave gave us our orders. "Mike and I will go in the front. You two," to Heck and Jean-Marc, "enter by the rear. We'll check out the restaurant. You guys case the bars - there're two of them. Don't let him see you. If he's there, we meet back here in ten minutes. If not, we still meet back here and then we go upstairs.

Beresford was not at dinner. Disappointed, Dave and I returned to the foyer. When Heck and Jean-Marc appeared a couple of minutes later we knew from their faces that they too had drawn a blank.

"We try his room. Mike, you stay here just in case. Heck. Use the lift. We'll take the stairs."

No consultation. Not that I minded. This time.

Not until, with Heck half way between floors two and three and Dave and Jean-Marc tripping up the stairs two at a time, Chris Beresford walked into the hotel and stood, with his back to me, well within knifing distance.

My heart lurched and my mouth dried up and I almost fouled Mr Hilton's nice marble floor. *Don't turn round*, I shrieked silently. *Don't see me!* I closed my eyes and when I opened them again he was gone.

My heart restarted and I scraped my tongue against the ridges of my lips. I felt suddenly calm. My confidence was restored - I had not done the toilet, had I? Should I follow the rat? He had either slipped outside again or else he had gone into the cocktail bar - there had not been time for him to have gone anywhere else.

Later, I'd use the house phone and call Room 369. Dave would be inside and he would answer the phone. "Hi, Dave," I'd say. "I've got him." He'd say, "Good work, Mike! Where are you?"

"In the foyer."

"And Beresford?"

"He's here too. Hog-tied - and ready to stand trial and then meet with summary execution!"

"Good work, Mike! We're on our way."

I galvanised myself into action and strode to the cocktail bar. I pushed the door to and peeped round it. No Beresford. Damn! He must have gone outside again. I returned to the main door and went out in time to see a Peugeot taxi pull away from the kerb. In the back seat was Christopher Beresford. He was grinning, evilly, at me and his right hand offered the Churchillian salute.

I ruffled my hair in frustration.   And preparation: I was suitably dishevelled when they burst out of the hotel. The three musketeers.

"Mike!"

"Mike!"

"Mike? Are you OK?"

I held my hand to my throat and gasped, "B . . . B . . . Beresford. It's Beresford! There! The taxi!" I pointed down Kenyatta Avenue where the fleeing cab blinked red lights. I slumped to my knees and held my head with both hands.

"Come on, for Crissakes! He's getting away!"

"Get up, ya big shite!"

It is at times of crises when you learn who your true friends are.

Dave and Heck raced for the car park and the Fiat. I thought that Jean-Marc hesitated but then he gave chase and I was left alone at the foot of the Leaning Tower of Nairobi, friendless. I went to follow but nobody was watching and so I repaired to the bar and dosed myself with the fruit of the vine in the guise of Remy Martin VSOP. After two gentleman's measures I felt a lot better. I'd never trust Americans again - had I ever? - or Belgians, and, of course, who ever had faith in twerps from the Gorbals?

I had switched to Tusker - brandy invariably makes me thirsty - by the time they returned. Failed again, I thought.

"You look pathetic," Heck muttered.

"I'm OK," I protested.

"We lost him." Dave snapped.

"I'm sorry," I apologised.

Suddenly, I had a thought.

"But I know where he's headed," I said.

"Back to Uganda," Dave said bitterly.

I hadn't thought of that. But I took a chance. "No!" I said.

"No?" someone said.

"No!" I declared. I took a sip of my beer (I wasn't well enough to glug it, was I?) and then, mindful of the boys, added, "You chaps want a drink?"

Dave sighed. And ordered a large Bourbon.

Jean-Marc wanted brandy and Heck was happy with a pint of Tusker and a double Johnny Walker Red Label and a bag of crisps.

They sipped and crunched and waited.

I said, "No."

They sipped and waited.

"I've been thinking," I explained. I could see it all so clearly. "Who came with passports?" I didn't wait for an answer. "Not Beresford, right? So. He's been escorted into Kenya by some Ugandan brigadier. But, the brigadier has gone home again. Of course he may have supplied Beresford with papers, but if he has, then they're here at the hotel. And he's not going to get them back, is he, Dave?"

Mercouri shook his head in agreement.

"So," I went on. "Beresford is now on his own. Oh, he'll have cash, but he knows that I at least have survived and am even now hot on his trail. So, whatever his original plans were, he's only got one course of action left to him."

I paused and glugged. Narrowed eyes awaited the guru's conclusion.

"He'll make for Mombasa and leave Kenya by sea. He'll go to the Seychelles."

Very simple.

Elementary.

They looked at me with respect and I remember thinking, it wasn't that remarkable, Holmes. Dave nodded slowly.

"Could be," he said.

CHAPTER 18

"Simba!"

The speaker was a Kikuyu clad in a khaki safari suit and he was pointing a long black finger at a bush ten feet from the open window of our Fiat 128.

Nice tree, I thought.

But I couldn't see any lions. And neither could Jean-Marc nor Heck from the back seat.

"Where - ?" I started to ask. The ranger placed his forefinger across his lips and, with his other hand, pointed into the heart of the bush.

"Simba," he repeated in a whisper.

And then, appearing as if by magic - like a colour photograph auto-developing after rolling from a Polaroid camera - the pride appeared from their camouflage. There were three lionesses, at least half a dozen cubs and, some twenty yards beyond the bush, a black-maned male which lay aloof, snoozing in the afternoon sun.

"Look at that big fucker at the back," Heck said in wonder - it was well seeing that Dave Mercouri was not with us. Dave had seen Africa's game often before and had stayed behind in the Voi Safari Lodge while we went out on the early evening run with our travelling ranger, Alun.

"If you want to see lion," Dave had said, "take a ranger. He'll know where to look. Simba tends to keep well off the main drag."

And so it had proved. Big Alun, who sweated even more freely than Heck, directed me - I had insisted on a turn at the wheel - off the murram track and into the savannah. We had already seen hippo and elephant and buffalo and a big black rhino that was grey. Now we were in lion country.

The females, their tawny hides flecked with droplets of blood collected at a recent meal, were content to nap. The cubs alone seemed to have any life about them and, once they grew accustomed to our presence, they cavorted in and around their bush. Occasionally one ventured too close to a sleeping mother or auntie. Only then did the adult stir and the savagery of her growls brought home to us that what we were watching were not overgrown tabby-cats. We watched and wondered for a long time until it was time to go.

But the car would not start. Not quite

accurate. It did start, but a heavy foot on the accelerator probably caused the engine to flood and cut out.

"Oh, well," I remarked as cheerfully as I could. "Not to worry. It'll start again in a minute."

Three quarters of an hour later the lions were still ten feet from our flooded, rapidly overheating and stationary car. Jean-Marc, as usual, took it quietly, like a man, but Heck, as usual, had plenty to say.

Only the ranger was smart enough to be afraid. Sweat lashed off his face. He realised that we were in extreme danger - nobody knew exactly where we were and there was only an hour or so till nightfall. He did not think of this expanse of grassland as a Park. These were the wilds of Africa and those cats snoozing quietly beside us were potential killers. He also knew that there was only one way to get the car started and he dreaded being the one to get out and push.

Without warning, he opened his door quietly and eased himself outside. Every few seconds he checked to see that the lions had not stirred. His action, with full knowledge, was brave; that of Heck and Jean-Marc was not especially so when, uninvited, they followed the ranger from the car. (I stayed put of course - well, somebody had to steer, hadn't I?) *We* thought of this grassland as a Park and did not believe that the cats were truly wild.

I engaged third gear as the Fiat started to roll down the slight gradient.

"Now!" Heck whispered.

I let out the clutch.

The car jerked forward but the engine did not start. We tried again and again but, although the engine turned over, the three men could not produce enough revs with their timorous pushing to get it to catch fully.

At the bottom of the slope was a swamp. I turned the wheel and the Fiat came to a standstill overlooking the mere. A number of crested cranes, Uganda's national bird, watched us as we watched the lions, now almost thirty yards off. Surely we were safe, I thought, for, even if a lion showed interest in us and ventured from the shade to investigate, the three would have plenty of time to scramble back inside the car.

Just then one of the lionesses roared. She did not apparently move, she merely roared. Merely! Hah! The sound came from deep in her belly and was terrifyingly loud, savage, primordial.

I jumped.

Heck jumped.

Jean-Marc jumped.

The ranger jumped.

They all jumped back into the car.

The lioness roared again. Only the ranger didn't look pale. The sound waves from the roar entered the car and reverberated shockingly in its cramped confines. I smiled nervously and looked at Alun for reassurance. The smile died on my lips. The perspiration our guide had exuded before was as nothing compared to the rivulets of sweat that now lashed down worry lines etched, no doubt, during situations such as this. Only now did we realise the enormity of the danger we were in.

Fortunately I remembered that I was the officer in charge. "Look, boys," I said, "if we can push the car over that little rise, the ground slopes again . . . . "

Heck gave me a venomous look. "If *we* can push again!" he muttered in disgust.

Alun grimaced. He was staring at the 'little rise' as if it were Mount Kilimanjaro, but he realised it was our only hope. He checked again the shade of the lions' den and, seeing that it had spilled out no inquisitive feline, edged once more from the car.

Heck and Jean-Marc followed. The extra distance from the pride gave them the confidence to push with grunts. The Fiat struggled over the hummocky crest.

"Right!" I exclaimed and the three men bent their backs and straightened their legs and the car shot forward.   I let out the clutch.   The engine roared.   I slammed on the brakes, found neutral and revved enthusiastically. The lads jumped back into the car and we headed for the lodge as the sun began to set.

****

Dave was waiting for us in the bar.

"Well?" he asked. "Did you see them?"

"See them!" Heck retorted, "we jest about moved in wi' them!" He launched into an account of our adventures and, of course, made much of my stalling the car. Fortunately, Dave did not understand most of what Heck was saying, and the edited version I gave later put the engine malfunction into proper perspective.

"What did you find out, Dave?" I asked. Dave hadn't been too keen to break our journey to the coast, but the rest of us, we converts to the Safari, had. Dave agreed because it gave him a chance to phone ahead and sound out his contacts in

Mombasa about the possible arrival in the port of Chris Beresford. He also realised how keen we were to see more game and especially lion and so he had consented to the overnight stay at Voi.

"Nothing definite," he replied. "But I've got people on the look-out at the docks. If he does try to get out of the country by sea, we'll have him. How's the throat by the way, Mike?"

I stroked my Adam's apple and was thankful that the flush in my cheeks was already there, sun-induced. "It's OK," I said.

"Good. And don't worry. It won't be long before it's your turn to put your hands around his throat. If," he added, "you're right about Mombasa."

CHAPTER 19

The next morning we were up at dawn and had our last look at the game of Tsavo. The waterhole was no more than thirty yards from a wide, wooden veranda that ran along one side of the lodge. We were all there as were another dozen or so of our fellow lodgers. Muted "ooohs" and "aaahs" announced the arrival of a mother elephant and her baby, a family of warthogs, a Thomson's gazelle. Cameras clicked with, to us, shocking loudness as a kudu bull drank alongside a splay-legged giraffe. We were at our last cocktail party in the savannah where carnivores drank with herbivores and were watched intently by omnivores, some of whom were planning what no animal has ever contemplated: an act of revenge.

As the sun rose higher the game dispersed and so did we. As I expected, I was forbidden the wheel. Heck took over the driving again and we set out on the last lap to Mombasa, a hundred miles to the east.

Mombasa is the capital of Coast Province and the chief port of Kenya. Sited on a coralline island in a coastal inlet of the Indian Ocean it is linked to the mainland by causeway, bridge and ferry. It was founded by Arab traders in the IIth century and, because of its strategic position, has been continually fought over by Arabs, Persians, Portuguese and Turks. In 1840 the Sultan of Zanzibar finally gained control of Mombasa. It came under British administration in 1895 and was capital of the East African Protectorate until 1907. All this information was gratuitously offered by Dave Mercouri from the back seat of the Fiat.

Mombasa has two ports: Old Mombasa Harbour on the island's east side and Kilindini Harbour to the west. The old port is now used only by dhows and small craft that bring trade from Arabia, the Persian Gulf and India (and, I assumed, allow fugitives to escape to the Seychelles).

We crossed to the island by the Makupa Causeway and made our way to the old quarter where, needless to say, Dave had friends. The old city is strongly oriental in character and has narrow streets and tall houses with curved ornamental balconies. Mosques and temples and bars abound. Dave settled us in one of the latter and went in search of information. He didn't invite us to accompany him and we were content to be left behind and have a couple of beers. The bar was a dump. A group of shifty-looking Arabs sat in a corner and at two other tables African men talked and drank and laughed loudly. The waitresses were very black and very flashily dressed and very available. They were also, very likely, very pox-ridden, but then, so, probably, was I. Heck's train of thought must have been along the same lines as my own: "Widn'ae touch them wi' a ten foot barge pole," he muttered.

Dave was back quicker than we expected - he returned while we were half way through our second beer. He shook his head in answer to our silent enquiries. "We wait," he said. "So I'll have a beer."

I signalled to a waitress and she brought four more glasses overflowing with foaming Tusker.

"We book into the Hotel Trianon," Dave continued. "If Beresford tries to leave by boat, Lawrence - that's my friend - will contact us there."

"Did we no' pass an airport back there?" Heck interrupted. "Mebbe he'll fly out?"

I shook my head. "No," I said with exaggerated patience. "Not without papers."

"He's got a gun, hasn't he?"

"I theenk 'Eck has ze point," Jean-Marc said.

Dave came to my rescue. "No," he said. "If he came here it wouldn't be to leave by air. The airport is only a small one - local flights only. I can't see him risking a show of force just to get back to Nairobi - where *we* might be waiting - or to go anywhere else in Kenya when a phone call would alert a reception committee. No, if he's come to Mombasa, he'll be planning to leave by sea, as Mike says." Dave emptied his glass. "Right," he said, "Let's get our asses over to the Hotel Trianon. Lawrence could be in touch at any time."

The Hotel Trianon was a doss-house that huddled in the shadow of Fort Jesus. Fort Jesus was a huge structure, built by the Portuguese in the sixteenth century. It was a museum now and looked in far better shape than the Hotel Trianon ever did or ever would.

We were in Mombasa three days. It was beginning to look like somebody had made a boo-boo. But then the word came through. I was the only one in the hotel bar when it did. Dave had dragged the other two off on a trip to the museum, but somebody had to man the phone and, as I had a headache (or so I said), it was left to me to hold my fort while they went to visit theirs.

The clerk was a shifty-looking cove who wore a left earring. "The phone," he told me. "It is for you." I laid down my book - "The Man-eaters of

Tsavo" - and carried my pint glass to the telephone.

"Hello? Who? Lawrence? No. Dave isn't here right now. Can I take a message? I'm King. Doctor King."

I listened carefully to Lawrence and experienced a mixture of emotions: satisfaction and surprise that I had guessed right; apprehension that a meeting was now imminent with the traitor - the karate black belt, fifth dan traitor; and fear when Lawrence said, "Doctor. You have very little time. Your, er, friend is at this moment boarding a craft bound for India."

The bastard!

Not only was he not going to the Seychelles, he was not going to the Seychelles *now!* And Mercouri and the others were at the museum, for God's sake! Lawrence had more to say.   "I can meet you for a couple of minutes and show you the boat if you come now.   Otherwise he'll be gone."

I explained that Dave would want to be there himself. "Couldn't you wait a little while - he's bound to be back soon - or I could go and fetch him?"

"Oh, *I* can wait OK but the boat won't - it's just about under way already.   So.   Do you come now or do we forget the whole thing?"

I was trapped. "Where?"

Lawrence directed me to the Pontoon Bridge that connects Mombasa to the Mainland; he would expect me in ten minutes. He rang off. I left a message for Dave with the clerk and asked him how far it was to the Pontoon Bridge.

"Oh, not far, suh. One mile. Not more.

A mile! Who did this guy Lawrence think I was? Roger Bannister? Then I thought: he'll think I've got a car. And so I had. But I didn't have the keys, did I? Heck had them tucked away safely in his trousers pocket.

"Can I get a taxi?" I asked the clerk.

"Oh yes, suh. Many, many taxis, just outside hotel."

I thanked him and ran for the door. Right enough, a taxi stood waiting twenty yards down the street.   I opened the back door and woke the driver up. "How much to the Pontoon Bridge?" I asked.

"Pontoon Bridge? Two hundred shillings."

"Two hundred!   I'll give you twenty."

The driver went back to sleep.

Didn't you think fifteen bucks was a small

price to pay? Dave would ask later when I told him I had missed Beresford.

"Here!" I threw two hundred shilling notes - my total allowance from Dave - into the front seat and heaved myself into the back. It wasn't my money anyway, was it? The African cabbie pocketed the cash and started up his motor. When we rocketed forward I felt a 10G force and knew that, barring accidents, I would be at the Pontoon Bridge in time to meet Lawrence and, perhaps, my nemesis.

Lawrence was an Irishman who had a part share in a bar somewhere on the waterfront. His partner, apparently, was a Kikuyu woman who actually ran the place while Lawrence mooched about making a few bob on the side.

"You King?" he asked as he held the door and I rolled, shocked, from the Peugeot-Ferrari taxi. I nodded. He didn't shake hands. He just jerked his head like he was Humphrey Bogart and, like Peter Lorre, I followed him meekly to the middle of the Pontoon Bridge. Lawrence was about five foot eight with brown hair and a cheerfully ugly face. He wore a filthy tee shirt, a pair of rugger shorts and green flip-flops that scraped the bridge as he shuffled along it.

He pointed to a cluster of boats moored

along the wharf. "That one there," he said and indicated a shabby twenty footer with a sail on top and a small outboard motor sticking out the back.

"Yer man's down below," he explained. "The Congola has a crew of two: that big Blackie in the bow and Indian Joe at the helm. Indian Joe's the skipper and he carries cargo - any cargo - as long as the money's right. It's a long way to Tipperary - or India - in a boat like that. Yer man must be desperate."

Yes, I thought, and he's not the only one. What was I going to do now that I had found "yer man"? First of all, King, enlist the help of the locals.

"What do we do now, Lawrence?" I asked.

"Sure I wouldn't have a clue," he replied cheerfully. "Me? I'm only the scout. Ye're on yer own, doc - but if I see Dave I'll be sure to tell him that you'll be needin' a hand."

With that, the little Irish bastard waved his dirty little paw and walked back off the bridge leaving me to plan and execute a naval battle when all I wanted to do was contemplate my own navel - preferably with the help of a bottle of Scotch.

I considered hollooing Beresford on the Congola and inviting him to surrender, but I rejected that scheme because, when he heard who was calling him, he would surely come out shooting. So what to do? Somehow I had to stop the damn boat from leaving. But how? I couldn't lasso it or rugby tackle it. So, what?

Indian Joe was now pulling on the engine's rip cord. It was bye-bye time. Maybe I could lasso *him*. Big Blackie in the bow leaned over and started to detach the painter that secured the boat to the wharf. I willed him to fall into the Indian Ocean but of course he did not oblige. Then, unexpectedly, Beresford came to the rescue himself.

I heard him before I saw him, but *he* surely saw *me* because he came out shooting. The first bullets whistled past my head - I could feel their wind. I dived for cover. Beresford fired again and again, but somehow I managed to get off the bridge unscathed and hide behind a big Ford Taunus parked nearby. Both Indian Joe and Big Blackie also took fright. The former fell backwards into the water while the Kenyan (he wasn't so keen now!) jumped ashore and took off.

I peeped through the windows of the Taunus and there he was. The traitor. His head and shoulders were all that were visible. And his gun, which he was reloading. I had done it. I had stopped him leaving Mombasa!

Suddenly the rest of him appeared from the bowels of the dhow. He was wearing a safari suit which I thought strange apparel for an ocean voyage, but an ocean voyage he was certainly determined to embark upon. He thrust his revolver down the waistband of his trousers and bent to the engine. I prayed for the gun to go off. He grasped the ripcord and pulled on it. Don't start, I pleaded. It did not start. He tried again and again but he didn't have the knack - the engine remained obstinately silent.

I prayed again, this time for deliverance. Where were they - Mercouri and the others? Surely they're still not at the bloody museum, I raged. They must have got my message by now. They should be here. And where were the police for God's sake? Somebody had just fired a million rounds in the middle of a city and no cavalry had seen fit to investigate!

Beresford tried the outboard once more, but when he was again frustrated, he hurled the toggle of the ripcord to the deck, kicked the motor, and scrambled ashore. The revolver appeared as if by magic in his hand. I knew that he was going hunting. He spied first Indian Joe who was pulling himself from the water about fifty yards downstream.

"Come back, you little bastard!" he yelled, but Indian Joe had other plans. Shaking himself like a nearly-drowned rat he sprinted off in pursuit of Big Blackie and was seen no more. Beresford went to follow him, but then he saw me and he clearly remembered that I was the game he was really after.

The next ten minutes were hilarious - straight out of a Marx Brothers' movie in fact. Beresford raced towards the Taunus, his gun at the ready. I knew that if I ran for it, he would shoot me down like a dog and so, while he went round to the driver's side of the car, I side-skipped the other way. He darted to the back; I drifted to the front. He went off-side; I crept to the driver's door. I could tell that he was getting annoyed. He tried shooting my head off over the car's roof but I foiled him by ducking. He fired at my feet under the vehicle but all he managed to shoot was the street and the undercarriage of the car.

"You'll hit the petrol tank!" I screamed and thankfully he saw the sense in my warning and stopped trying to blow us up.

Frustration and feeling foolish rather than fatigue probably pulled him up. Me? I was exhausted and terrified.

"You'll never get away, Beresford," I wheezed.

He grinned evilly. I wondered why. Then I

saw what he planned. He yanked on the driver's door. It was unlocked. He got into the car, slid into the passenger's seat and opened the other door, hoping no doubt to catch me napping and then shoot me in the stomach. But I was too quick for him. While he was making sure that the gear lever didn't do him any permanent damage I skipped to the rear of the car and peeked in at him through the back window. He shot it (the back window) out and probably deafened himself in the process. It was stalemate and he knew it.

He got out of the car again and stood uncertainly in the middle of the road. I wondered how much ammunition he had left. I didn't have to wonder for long. As I crouched at the corner of the car boot a cramp suddenly struck my left leg. In a reflex action I stood upright to relieve the pain and, thus exposed, looked into Beresford's cruel eyes and the barrel of his revolver. He fired.

Click.

He fired again.

Click.

His gun was empty.

My cramp was gone. I laughed out loud. When he threw the gun into the water I laughed again. No more ammo at all! I stopped laughing when he edged his hands and started round the car again after me. I had seen what those "hands of death" could do to a pile of bricks and had no illusions as to what they could do to my spinal cord.

Round and round we went. He was getting very annoyed.

"You can't be on your own, King," he snarled over the bonnet of the car.

"Why not?" I asked. (That's the boy, Mikey. Keep him talking.)

"Because you don't have the gumption to have found me. You needed help."

I shrugged. Play it cool, Mike boy. Don't let him get to you.

"So who else escaped? Snyder? No. I heard that they got Snyder. Mercouri then. That's right. Mercouri was with you. What happened - you arrive too late for the party?"

While Beresford talked he started on a new ploy. He climbed on the bonnet and then on to the roof of the car. He took time there to leer down at my inferior status. The stalemate was broken and he knew it. I knew it too and the only reason I was not off like a scalded cat on anabolic steroids was that, between Beresford's legs, I suddenly espied a friendly Fiat about to knock off his left testicle. A couple more minutes. That was all that was needed.

"Why did you do it, Chris?" I asked in the earnest way I have of enquiring after the health of rich patients. He didn't answer. Instead, he launched himself from the car roof. I did not flinch. Surprised, he checked. He looked into my eyes. I looked over his shoulder as Mercouri and Heck and Jean-Marc piled out of the Fiat and, guns drawn, approached like the Earps at the OK Corral.

Beresford looked round. He blanched. Then, with an oath, he made to trample over me and yet leave me in the line of fire of the avenging mercenaries.

Déjâ vu. Once before. At school in Gosforth. I had been coerced into turning out for the rugby fifteen of the class below mine. I had got myself into the worst possible position: isolated in defence where to shirk the tackle would have been seen, especially by younger boys, as arrant cowardice. The no-alternative tackle. I had been forced to take it on then in the north of England and I did so again now on the Island of Mombasa.

I took him low. He took me high. As my arms gripped his calves his knee followed through and slammed against my mouth. In reaction, and completely in accordance with Newton's Third Law of Motion, my lower incisors tore through my bottom lip and ripped into his knee-cap. I collapsed. He fell on top of me. Heck fell on him and persuaded him to release his grip on my neck by employing the simple expedient of slipping around his neck the deadly garrotte to which he had added toggles.

I heard a click. I opened my eyes. Mercouri had cocked his revolver, the barrel of which was now pressed against Beresford's temple. We all got up and while Beresford spat out invective most hurtful, I spat out blood.

"Well done, Mike boy," Dave said. "You OK?"

I touched my lip with tender fingers and shrugged. (I couldn't risk saying anything in case I burst into tears.)

Beresford was bundled into the car and made to lie on the floor in the back under the feet of Heck and Jean-Marc. Dave drove and I bled beside him. The next scene to unfold would be the trial. We had planned, if not rehearsed, for this. Beresford was to be tried by a Judge Jeffries who was keen on swing even before Sinatra. Then he would be executed.

CHAPTER 20

We used for our courthouse an upstairs room in Lawrence's pub. Except it wasn't a pub. It was a brothel and Mama Lawrence was not too happy about one of her rooms being used for a purpose other than its designated one. Until Dave pressed 500 bob into her podgy palm and patted her on the head. "If we take longer than what the room would earn," he told her, "you let me know, huh, Mama?"

Mama Lawrence beamed then. She was about four feet six and had iron grey hair to match the rod with which she ruled her house. The girls were terrified of her. Lawrence had not turned up yet - it seemed that he liked to do his early evening drinking elsewhere in town.

The furnishings of the room were sparse: a bed, a hard-backed chair and a rickety wardrobe that was ancient but would never be antique. We pushed the bed against the wall and sat Beresford on the chair at its foot. Finally, we commandeered other chairs and placed three of them in a row against the wall opposite the "dock".

It had been agreed that Jean-Marc would preside as judge, that Dave would be prosecutor and that I would be defending counsel. I had protested of course. "I can't defend," I told Mercouri. "I have no conviction that the prisoner is innocent."

"Good," Dave replied. "There's only one conviction we want here - but we'll go through the motions anyway."

Then I remembered my torn lip. In fact, the tunnel carved by my teeth had taken no time to start to heal - the outer opening was sealed already and the inner gash was closing fast. "I can't talk properly," I mumbled

"Then you won't have much to say, will you?"

And so it was settled.

Heck was to keep the prisoner covered and blow his head off if he made a wrong move. He volunteered for more than a guard's job, however. "Ah'll be the executioner," he announced with relish, "when the time comes."

Dave opened the proceedings.

"Your Honour," he said.   "The prosecution contends that, about a month ago - "

"Objection, Your Honour," I interrupted, "We

are dealing with a man's life here. *About* a month ago is hardly specific enough. I suggest - "

I stopped. Dave was staring at me coldly. He had already, it seemed, given the nod to Heck because my little countryman had swung his pistol away from Beresford. It now covered me. Methought I protested too much.

"About a month ago," Dave repeated without fear of interruption, "Christopher Beresford, a member of our band of . . . er . . liberators, sold us down the river to Idi Amin. He ain't nuts, he did it for dough and I demand a verdict of guilty."

He sat down only to stand up again. "The prosecution rests," he added.

Jean-Marc coughed. "Monsieur le defense?" he murmured.

I was on. But what was I going to say? Couldn't just say nothing. Had to give Beresford the semblance of a fair trial. I got to my feet.

"Your Honour," I said. (I did toy with the idea of addressing the court as "m' lud", but changed my mind at the last moment.) "As I have had no opportunity to confer with my . . . er . . . client, I wish to ask for a stay - for an adjournment - so that proper consultation can take place."

I sat down again.

Heck laughed out loud. "You must be jokin'," he said.

Dave smouldered.

Jean-Marc said, "Request, she is denied."

So that was that.

I looked at my client and shrugged. He returned the look and added contempt to the disinterest that he had not tried to hide since the charade had begun.

"It's a load of balls!" he snarled. "This isn't a court - it's a fiasco. I refuse to take part in this . . . this . . . . mockery!"

"Ye'll no' be needed," Heck reminded him, "till the last act."

Beresford's lip curled but he said no more. Counsel for the defence rose to his feet for a second time. I marshalled my thoughts, composed my features, gripped my lapels and began.

"Your Honour. After careful, if hurried deliberation, and a minimum of consultation, my client and I have decided to plead guilty as charged - well, what I mean is, *he* is pleading guilty. We realise that the evidence is overwhelmingly against our - his - case and we accept that there is no way that he can beat the rap"

I paused and surveyed my listeners. The judge was smoothing his van Dyke and nodding gravely; Heck was picking his left nostril for a change; Dave was yawning and my client smouldered. Not encouraged, I nevertheless stuck to my task.

"My plea is one of mitigation and I cite the defendant's first, if obvious, disadvantage: he is Welsh and, as such, can hardly be expected to display loyalty to those of a nationality other than his own."

I couldn't resist it - I'm sometimes blinded by my prejudice against the Druids! My barb, however, fell on stony ground because only Heck semi-appreciated the jibe and he didn't count.

"Christopher Beresford," I went on, "spent a month at the camp in England preparing us - and preparing us well - for our mission in Uganda. There is no evidence that he was planning his treachery - his deal with Amin - during those early days -"

"Yeah?" Dave interrupted. "So when did he make the deal? When he was parachuting down?"

Heck guffawed. "Nice one, Major," he laughed.

I appealed to Judge Jean-Marc.

"I appeal to Your Honour," I said.

"Appeal. She is denied,"

I was speechless, not at the judicial decision, but rather because I had no speech to deliver. What I needed was a witness.

"Your Honour," I said. "I would like to call the defendant to the stand, and if he refuses to be called, I would like to rest my defence and throw my client at the mercy of the court."

I sat down thinking that where I really wanted to throw him was out of the window. Jean-Marc considered my request in a silent courtroom and when there were no objections he granted his permission.

"OK ," he said.

I allowed Beresford a decent interval of time to refuse to take the stand.

Silence.

"Are you guilty or not guilty?" I asked, thinking that perhaps he should have been asked this earlier.
"Have you anything to say before the court passes sentence?" I asked this last question, but the look I got from Jean-Marc left me in no doubt that he

thought it should have come from the bench.

"' Ave you anything to say before ze
court   passes sentence?"

Beresford treated us in turn to looks that were
pure cyanide. He closed his eyes and I thought that
he was going to remain silent, but then his reserve
cracked.

"You hypocrites!" he spat. "You fucking
hypocrites! You set yourselves up in a kangaroo
court and pretend a righteousness that is pathetic.
You sell yourselves and your guns and," he sneered,
"your syringes in an enterprise that was doomed
from the start - just like your abortive coup in the
Seychelles. You're amateurs! Bunglers!"

And then he made his bid for freedom. He
catapulted from his chair and dived across the room.
Heck tried to shoot him but, instead of firing, his gun
went "click" - it had jammed - or was empty.
Beresford reached him before we could react and
dealt him a *mowashi-ampi* - a forearm elbow strike
to the head that flattened him. The little Glaswegian
lay still. Dave and Jean-Marc sprang forward.
Pivoting on one foot, Beresford lashed out with his
other leg in an *amawashigeri* - a round-house kick
that caught the Belgian on the chest. Jean-Marc
was flung backwards. His head bounced off the wall
and he too slumped to the floor. Dave grappled with

Beresford and tried to pin his arms to his side. The Englishman rolled from Dave's grip and the two men circled one another with their hands edged.

Beresford kicked off his shoes. Mercouri did not. Dave was pretty good at the old karate, but I didn't think that he was a match for Beresford. Neither did Dave because he pulled his gun from his trousers pocket and levelled it at Beresford's head.

"Lie down on the floor, scum, or I'll blow your head - "

Beresford didn't wait for Dave to finish his sentence. He unleashed a second *mawashi-geri* that spun the revolver from Dave's grasp and followed up with a strike with the back of his fist - a *uraken* - that missed by a whisker. I dodged to the side to give them space, but Dave misconstrued my movement.

"Keep out of this, Mike!" he growled. "He's mine."

Dave must have had second thoughts about his chances or else he had just become awfully mad. Beresford was a black belt, fifth dan. Mercouri held a black belt too, but he had not progressed formally beyond the second dan stage. On paper Beresford should have won hands down, but then, they weren't fighting on paper.

The two men grappled and fell heavily, but they were soon on their feet again and circling each other with extreme caution. There was little of the exaggerated posing of Inspector Clouseau and his valet in Pink Panther movies; but each was ready to kill and the other knew it.

I left them to it and went to check on my two fallen comrades. Jean-Marc was stirring already and would suffer from no more than a bump on the head sustained when he collided with the wall. Heck was still unconscious, but he was breathing deeply and regularly and his prognosis was not too terrible either.

When I looked back, I saw that Dave and Beresford were getting into a dreadful muddle. I had never understood karate - give me a good old-fashioned boxing match any day. They fought with a ferocity that was all the more grim because they engaged in silence. I had expected Japanese war whoops, but the only eastern menace they showed was a slanting of their eyes as they took each other's measure. Feet and hands flashed but, if you ask me, precious few blows actually connected with their intended targets.

Dave's gun had been kicked to the side of the room. I sidled round to it, picked it up and cocked it. Insurance, I thought. At one stage the adversaries fell on to the bed. They thrashed around and I was sure that it was going to collapse but it didn't, and when you come to think about it, are such pieces of furniture in cat houses not built for action?

Suddenly, Dave shot backwards from the bed with blood spewing from his nose. Chris Beresford leapt after him and this time he accompanied his advance with a blood-curdling *kya* that said *'I'm going to bleak you fucking oliental neck!'* Dave tripped over Heck's outstretched feet and Beresford closed in for the kill.

It was time for me to step in. I gripped the revolver butt tightly and took the two necessary paces to where the traitor was about to deliver his *coup de grace*. I raised the gun and made to knock Beresford on the head. His edged hand fell at the same time as did mine. His impetus carried him forward and I missed him with my cosh. But not with the gun. The revolver suddenly went off and Beresford, minus the top of his head, lurched forward and fell on top of his intended victim. King had saved the day and had also, inadvertantly, proved to be an able deputy for Heck in the role of executioner.

The silence after the gun's roar was palpable. It was broken by a female voice coming from the corridor.

"What is happening? What is happening?"

Dave looked up at me from the floor with a mixture of gratitude and irritation. "Get rid of her!" he snapped.

I opened the door a crack. Mama Lawrence stood in the hallway with a delicious little black girl who in different circumstances . . . . . .

"It's all right," I said with a disarming smile. "Nothing to worry about. My friend was cleaning his rifle and it just went off. Sorry if it disturbed you."

Mama Lawrence watched me through slitted eyelids. "I no want trouble," she said. "You go soon. All of you."

I nodded. "We're on our way. Very soon, OK?"

I must say her reaction took me by surprise. It wasn't that she had *objected* to the noise, but that she had done so in such a calm manner. Then, I suppose, strange things happen not infrequently in these waterside brothels and the neighbours would not be expected to object too much. I smiled again and retreated into the room of execution.

The theatre of execution. Or the operating theatre, judging from the number of casualties draped around the room. Dave's craggy face was now more rugged than before, sporting as it did a broken nose that still dripped blood. He removed the handkerchief with which he tried to staunch the flow and I examined his wound.

"It'll be tender for a while," I grunted, "but you'll live."

He thanked me dryly.

Jean-Marc was up and about and, of course, neither complained nor required attention. (How do you treat a brick shit house with an easter egg on the back of his head anyway, for God's sake?)

"How's Heck?" Dave asked.

The little Glaswegian was stirring. There was an angry weal on the side of his neck that suggested he had been half hung - hanged. He sat up and caressed his injury. Dave and I helped him to his feet.

"It's a pity he didn't catch you on the head," I told him cheerfully. "That way, the damage would have been to him."

Heck glowered. "Where is the bastard?" he asked.

I nodded towards Beresford's body and Heck said, "Oh, did ah dae that tae 'im?"

"Not exactly," Dave laughed. "He was about to finish me off when the good doctor took a hand."

I shrugged modestly and tried not to be sick. The appearance of the top of Beresford's brain brought home to me that I had just killed a man - my first.

"We're going to have to get him out of here," Dave said through his broken nose.

I nodded. "That's what Mama Lawrence said."

Dave took a wad of banknotes from his hip pocket. He peeled off several and handed them to me. I didn't think it was my reward for saving his life and I was right.

"See if Papa Lawrence has arrived," Dave ordered. "If he hasn't, tell Mama that we're going to have to borrow one of her blankets - pay her for it. Tell her we'll be gone as soon as it's dark."

As I left the room Dave was already stripping the blanket from the bed while Jean-Marc was laying out the corpse for enshrouding.

I found Mama Lawrence just round the bend in the corridor. She was flanked now by a trio of beauties who cowered behind their employer and who had obviously been ordered to be in attendance. Lawrence, apparently, had still not yet returned. I gave his wife the cash and explained about the blanket. She asked no questions; she just accepted the money and, tightlipped, suggested that, when we went, we used the back door. I had her tell me the best route from the front to the rear of the house and then, having returned to collect the keys from Dave, moved the car to the back entrance.

I locked up and went back into the house where Beresford was all wrapped up and ready for his final journey. We carried him in quatro - one to each limb - and dumped him in the boot. We left without saying goodbye and drove in silence back over the Causeway and on to mainland Kenya. We considered a watery grave for Beresford, but decided that that was too good for him. We eventually laid him to rest - well, we tossed his body into a bush about half a mile from the main road at a spot where we saw hyenas. We hoped there were jackals around too. And vultures. Then we drove on to Nairobi.

CHAPTER 21

We said goodbye to Dave Mercouri at Heathrow just before he boarded his Pan Am flight to New York.

"Maybe I'm a jinx," I suggested. I hate farewells and I always come out with some banality or other just to fill the awkward silences. "It's been one disaster after another since I joined up."

I waited for him to refute this and was somewhat miffed when he did not do so immediately. But his silence was only a tease.

"No jinx, Mike," he told me with a grin. "The disasters, from the lack of funding in the Seychelles to Beresford's treachery in Uganda, would have happened anyway. Although," he added, "you didn't help matters - certainly not blood-pressure-wise - when you took a hike in Kampala."

I could have pointed out quite a few other instances when my actions might have spelt calamity for the group but, of course, I didn't. What Dave Mercouri didn't know wouldn't hurt him and besides, I had no desire to disillusion a friend who thought that I was other than a disaster area.

When we had got back to Nairobi, Jean-Marc had presented himself at the Belgian embassy while Heck visited the British High Commission. Each reported the loss of his passport. Each was promised action and, indeed, within the week, both men were provided with replacement documents which enabled them to get home. We had all flown to Zurich, done the business at the Credit Suisse Bank and had a celebration the same night which I am assured went like a bomb; the details of that night were doubtlessly lodged in the millions of my brain cells destroyed by a surfeit of Lowenbrau and Cardhu.

From Switzerland, Jean-Marc flew home to Brussels while Heck, Dave and I headed for London. Dave then caught his connection to the States, leaving Heck and me alone in the Smoke. At first Heck was all for an immediate journey north, but when he found out that I had business to attend to in London, he displayed his usual tact and good taste by asking, "What's that then?" and adding, "Ye'll be wantin' a fuckin' hand ah suppose."

We were sitting in the upstairs bar in Terminal 1. My first impulse was to decline his offer, but then I thought, why not? Finding a missing person would be quicker with two searching. But what would I tell him? I couldn't tell him the truth. The little bastard would laugh. Then I thought, what the hell! And so I told him about the casino and the money and Natasha. The little bastard laughed. I thought he was going to bust a gut. I wished he *would* bust a gut. I *knew* I shouldn't have told him.

"Fuck me," he gurgled. "'Twelve thou a screw!   Hee! Hee! Hee!"

When he stopped laughing about two pints later he said, "Right, Mike son. This is fuckin' serious. We're gonny huv' tae find the bitch. D'ye ken where she'll be?"

I didn't take umbrage and walk out. I was close to it - very close - but when he called me "son" I had to give him another chance. Let me tell you about being called "son". Mothers do it. And fathers. John Wayne does it. But when a Scotsman does it to another man – especially an Englishman – it means that that person is respected and liked. Age does not come into it - I've heard 25 year old men calling sixty year olds "son" as a term of endearment; it is not used lightly. It did not mean that I was Heck's son - like in filial offspring. It meant that he didn't think after all that I was just a lump of shite and this, hot on the heels of what Dave Mercouri had intimated to me, was heady stuff.

"There are two possible starting places," I told Heck. "The Hotel Belvedere and the Casino. If we

draw a blank there we're going to have problems -
the name she's using is Mrs Smith, remember."

We drove our hired car back into London and
booked into the Belvedere. I made discreet
enquiries at reception about a Mrs Smith who had
stayed in the hotel a couple of months before. The
receptionist was friendly and eager to please, but all
she could tell us was that, recently, seven Mr Smiths
had stayed in the hotel; so had four Mr and Mrs
Smiths, two Miss Smiths and one Sir Geoffrey
Smythe. I described *my* Mrs Smith to her, but she
could not put a face to the name or vice versa. She
did promise, however, to ask around and if she
learnt anything about my missing lady, she would
pass the information on to me posthaste.

"The Casino," I said to Heck as we made our
way disconsolately to the bar. "After dinner."

"Aye," he replied. "An' mebbe ye kin gie me
some lessons in roulette. Ye must huv a system,
eh?"

I shook my head. "Not exactly," I told him.

"Ye mean ye were jist fuckin' lucky?"

"Well, if you want to put it like that."

"Ye ken whit they say about lightning?"

234

"Oh yes. But I'm not going to gamble tonight. If she's not there we'll - " I stopped short.   What *would* we do if   she wasn't there?

"We'll think o' somethin'," Heck muttered. "Now. Whit are ye drinkin'?"

After a couple of snifters and a good meal we drove to the Cardinal Casino. As we walked from the car park I was filled with a terrible foreboding.   I couldn't explain it. I just knew that she was going to be there and that something dreadful was going to happen.   Perhaps . . . oh no, not that . . . *perhaps she would already be at the tables.   She   would   look gorgeous and I would feel like forgiving her. Her hair would shimmer like the jewels she wore that my money had paid for and forgiveness would go out the window. Her eyes would be   bright and full of allure and greed. She would be betting maximum amounts.   She would not see me. She would bet on the zero. Twenty four would come up. She would smile wistfully and   the gigolo beside her would shake his head sadly.   "Too   bad,   my dear," he would say. "That brings your losses to twenty five thou."*

"Yes," she would reply. "And now I am broke,"

No! Please! Not that!

The commissionaire held the door for us. I signed Heck in and hoped that he would behave himself. The gambling hall was quiet - it was only ten o'clock - and a glance told us that she was not there. We had planned to give her till two in the morning and so, to kill some time, we went for a drink.

When we were seated in the bar with large whiskies in front of us, I asked my companion, "How much money did you bring with you?"

"A coupla hundred," he grunted. "How about you?"

"About the same. Do you fancy a flutter?"

"I thought ye werenae gonny bet the night."

"I wasn't. It's just that, we may have quite a while to wait - if she comes at all. It would pass the time."

"Aye, a' right then," he said.

He was easily persuaded. We each bought £100 worth of chips and agreed to share any winnings. We split up and, while Heck tried his luck at roulette, I had a go at blackjack. In ten minutes I had lost ten quid and, bored with the game, wandered over to see how my partner was faring.

Heck was nowhere to be seen. I scanned again the roulette tables and then the blackjack counters. No Heck. I looked into the alcoves where bandits winked enticingly but the bandit for whom I searched was not there. He's gone to the toilet, I thought. Better check. The urinals were empty and only one cubicle had a closed door.

"Are you in there, Heck?" I whispered.

No reply.

"Heck!" I tried again.

An unfamiliar voice replied in exasperation, "Christ! Can a man not be left in peace to have a shit!"

Covered in confusion, I retreated from the men's room before I was spotted and went to check at the bar. Heck wasn't there but the barman was and so I had a whisky.

Where had he gone? Had he found his way into a private room where the high rollers play? Surely not. Not with a measly hundred quid. I finished my drink and checked again the gambling hall and the toilets. Zilch. I returned to the lounge and asked the barman if there were any other rooms in the casino that were open to members - maybe Heck had gone to watch television. The barman said that there were no further public apartments.

I took a final dram across to a corner table and began to worry sitting down. A redhead with piercing green eyes flapped them over her escort's bald head, but I didn't return the flap - I was in too much of one of my own and besides, once bitten . . .

While I sat thinking, an enormous man in evening dress came into the bar. He went straight up to the counter, said something to the barman who nodded in my direction. Then he strode over to my table. As this tuxedoed tyrannosaurus rex approached, I involuntarily placed my hand into my inside pocket. I was unarmed of course, but I thought that if the newcomer was hostile he might believe that I carried a gun and he might think twice before picking me up and throwing me out of the window. My training had taught me to expect the unexpected. Or so I thought.

Man-mountain halted at my table and, in a ludicrously piercing falsetto, said, "Doctor King?" Disarmed, and very surprised, I nodded up at him. How could he have possibly known - ?

"Your friend, Professor Laplace, wishes to speak with you most urgently."

"Who?" I asked.

"Professor Laplace - Professor *Hector*

Laplace - the Nobel Prize winner - he asks for you on the telephone."

Professor Laplace. Professor *Hector* Laplace! *Hector*! Heck! What the heck - what the hell - was going on?

"Oh. *That* Professor Laplace!" I said. "Very kind of you to come and . . . Where - ?"

"This way, Doctor Loltup."

Goliath turned and led the way - I had to run to keep up with hin - to a door that bore a notice: "Assistant Manager. Mr Marx." I was shown inside. Groucho - or was it Karl? - pointed to the phone and dipped out of the room again so that I could speak in private to my professorial colleague!

"Heck?" I whispered into the handset. "Is that you?"

A heavily accented - French accented - voice replied.

"But of course it is moi! 'Oo do you expect?"

I had forgotten that Heck could speak French.

"What the - "

"I've seen her!" he interrupted in his more

familiar, incoherent drawl - good cover, I thought, should anybody be listening in.

"You've seen - ?"

"Yer friend.   The one wi' the big . . . bank balance!"

"Natasha! You've seen Natasha!" (So much for security!) "Where? Where are you for God's sake?"

"Ah'm lookin' at her right now. Ah'm in the Trafalgar Hotel. Ah kin see her through the gless in this booth. She's huvin' a drink. Ye better get yer arse over here and then ah'll tell ye a' about it!" He hung up.

I assumed that Heck had taken the car in his pursuit of Natasha (he *had* driven to the casino and he did have the keys) and so I hailed a taxi. Ten minutes later I was dropped off at a large, modern building, the Hotel Trafalgar. Heck was waiting outside. I paid off the cabbie and joined the little Glaswegian who stood well to the side of the hotel's double glass doors.

"Give," I demanded, "*Professor!*'

He grinned. "You had disappeared," he began. "Ah wis playin' roulette. And in she marched. As bold as brass. Ye were right, Mike,

240

she's a whole lot o' woman! That wis the good news. Now the bad."

"Go on then."

"She saw you. At the blackjack table. Ye were side-on tae her but the way she went pale telt me that, not only wis it her, but also that she had ye spotted."

"So? What did she do?"

"She scarpered. Jest aboot-turned and shot the craw as fast as she could wi'oot runnin'. Ah hud nae time tae warn ye. So ah followed her. Here."

I warmed to Heck even more at that instant and nearly called him "son".

"Well done, Heck" I congratulated. "You did a grand job. So where is she now?"

"Jest after ah finished talkin' tae you, she finished her drink and left the bar. She got her key and went up," he thumbed the sky, "in the lift."

"I don't suppose you managed to get - "

"Room four-oh-seven - ah saw the number in her pigeon hole when the gadgie gied her her key."

"Excellent! Excellent, Heck! Now, was she alone?"

"She wis on her ain in the bar, but upstairs, ah dinae ken. She might have another mug tucked away up there."

I looked at him with distaste. Why did he have to go and spoil it? *Another* mug, indeed!

"Whit d'ye want to dae?" he asked.

Another decision. On this occasion, however, I was ready. "We go up there," I told him, "and I get my money back."

Heck looked doubtful. "She's no likely tae huv' it a' on her in cash. Ye're no' thinkin' o' takin' a cheque, are ye?"

"Don't be daft!" I snapped. "This is what we do. We put the frighteners on her and then never let her out of our sight until she can go to the bank or where ever she's got the money stashed and hand it over. Then we'll see."

"Aye, right," he said.

Room 407 was on the third floor. I took the elevator and, to be on the safe side, Heck went up the stairs. He was waiting for me in the corridor when the lift doors opened. He was trying not to breathe hard. "Whit kept ye?" he asked with a grin.

I ignored his cheek and looked for door

numbers.

"Four-oh-seven's doon here," he said and started off down the corridor. I followed. He stopped at a large trolley heaped with items that are replaced often in hotel bedrooms. He draped a pair of towels over his arm and continued on to room 407.

"Keep out o' sight," he ordered and at the same time knocked on the door.

"Who is it?" a voice I thought I recognised said.

"Room service," Heck replied in his exaggerated French accent. "Your towels, Madame."

There was a pause. Then the door was unlocked from the inside and it opened a crack. A crack was wide enough for Heck. He placed his shoulder against the panels and pushed. The door gave. Heck hurtled into the room and bowled over its occupant. She started to call out but her scream was stillborn as Heck smothered her face in his towels and pushed her to the floor. By the time I got in he was lying on top of her. She was outstretched on the carpet with her legs open like they had been the last time I saw her. Her skirt had ridden up her thighs and her underwear was black. I recognised the mole at the top of her left leg before I caught a glimpse of her face.

"Dinnae make a sound," Heck whispered fiercely, "and ah'll take away the towels."

The head behind the cotton nodded vigourously. Heck removed the cloth. Right enough it was Natasha. She focussed on Heck, looked past him, saw me and screamed. Or started to. Her mouth was immediately filled with towel and she gagged.

I closed the door and said, "Natasha, calm down. We are not going to hurt you. We just want to talk. Now, when my friend removes the towels this time, you will stay quiet. Otherwise he will cosh you. Is that understood?"

Vigorous nod.

"Right, Heck", I ordered. "Let her go. But be ready with the hammer."

Cautiously Heck, still astride Natasha's stomach, pulled back the towels. The woman's face was scrubbed clean of make-up and her lines showed - she had obviously been getting ready for bed just before we dropped in. One breast had popped out of her bra and her nipple peeped up at us like a hazel nut in a sea of blancmange. Heck allowed her to get up but when she made to rearrange her dress he shook his head. She let her hands drop into her lap. He waved her on to a nearby chair. It was time I took control - I was the officer, was I not, and it *had* been my money!

"It's been a long time, Natasha," I began. "I've missed you."

She made no reply. She was watching Heck who had taken from his pocket Dave Mercouri's garrotte. He had made a simple loop in the wire and slipped into it a bar of soap obtained from the suite's bathroom. As I was telling Natasha how much I had missed her, Heck was pulling tightly on his wire. The soap split in two and the fragments spilled on to the floor. Natasha watched with horror. When she looked up, Heck was staring at her unprotected breast and he was making another loop in his garrotte. He looked down at it, then back to her breast. Natasha got the message and shivered.

"I . . . I . . ." she stammered.

"It's my money, you see," I told her quietly. "I want it back. *We* want it back. All of it. Twenty-five thousnd pounds."

"I . . . I . . ."

"Where is it, Natasha?" I continued with more menace.

Natasha wrenched her gaze from the garrotte

and stared at me. "You're not going to believe this, Mike - "

"Try me."

"I . . . I . . . haven't got it."

I had an awful feeling that, not only was she going to say that, but also that it was going to turn out to be the truth. As yet, however, I was far from convinced. Neither was Heck.

"Mebbe if ah snip off her nipple, she'll remember where she put it," he suggested.

I shuddered inwardly but kept my face expressionless. "Is that how you want it?" I demanded.

She shook her head. "You don't understand," she wailed. "I know where it is. I just don't have it anywmore. "I . . . I . . . ."

"Well?"

"I lost it at the casino."

She started to cry.

"Ye're a fuckin' liar!"

"I'm not! I'm not! You can ask at the casino. They'll tell you!"

Heck took a step towards the frightened woman, but I signalled him to stop. Surprisingly, he did.

"Where is your purse?" I demanded.

She pointed to the sideboard on top of which rested a black leather handbag. I picked it up and emptied its contents into the bole of one of the sitting room's easy chairs. Besides combs and brushes and lipsticks and God knows what else, there was a chunky black purse which I opened. It contained £12 in one pound notes, a white button and a set of three keys.

"You wouldn't have got far in the casino with this," I remarked.

"I was hoping to meet . . . "

"Another mug!" Heck interrupted.

"A . . . a . . benefactor."

"What are the keys for?"

"Nothing much."

"They're car keys."

"If you call a 1965 Ford Cortina a car. Yes, I suppose so."

"What about that one?" I held up the third key in the bunch: a silver one with a number on it.

"Oh that," she said carelessly. That's just the key to my old locker at the Golf Club - "

"Yeah? Which Golf Club?"

"The Norton Park."

"Here in London?"

"Yes."

"Never heard of it."

"Well, it's not one of the more fashionable - "

"Whit's in it?"

"The locker?"

"Naw! The Taj Mahal!"

"Just an old set of golf clubs - and a pair of spiked shoes."

"Where are your credit cards - and cheque book?"

"I don't use them."

"Only cash, eh?"

She nodded.

"Where's your suitcase?"

"In the bedroom - in the wardrobe."

"Ah'll get it."

Heck returned with a brown leather suitcase and, while Natasha sat quaking, we went through her things - all of them. There were no letters, no bank books, no receipts. And there was no money. There was, however, some jewellery.

"You can take that," she said.

Heck grinned evilly. "Thanks a bunch," he said, "but it's no' a' we'll be takin'!"

What little confidence had returned to Natasha's face drained away again. I wondered what Heck meant. I was confused and when I'm confused I act on impulse. Sometimes the action removes the embarrassment. Sometimes . . .

"That key is not for the Norton Park Golf Club," I heard myself saying. Natasha donned her poker face. "There *is* no Norton Park Golf Club!" I went on implacably. Her facade crumbled. Her eyes dodged mine. And then I knew. "You've got the cash stashed away," I accused. "in a safety deposit box. And that's the key!"

Heck looked on with admiration - well, his mouth was open and so I suppose the stupid expression on his face *could* have hidden an admiring glance. Natasha was holding her head in her hands. She had started to cry again. "No, no," she wailed between sobs. "It's for the Golf Club."

Heck zinged his garrotte by twirling it fast through the air. She didn't need to lift her head to search for the source. She looked like a caged cat - a tigress, maybe, or a lynx.

"What bank?" Heck demanded.

Natasha stopped snivelling. A look of resignation came over her face and she shrugged. Sharing her cash, she was no doubt thinking, was better than sliced left breast à la garrotte.

"All right," she said in a manner more controlled than before. "All right. You've sussed it, Mike. It's not a Golf Course key. But it isn't a bank key either. It's for a . . . post-office box. But before I tell you which one, we're going to have to make a deal."

Heck snorted. "Ye're in no position tae be makin' deals!' he snarled.

Natasha turned her palms up and appealed directly to me. "Now listen," she said. "It's true that I have a little money left but I want some too - or I tell you nothing. I want half. If I lose everything I might as well be dead and so if you don't agree you'll have to kill me or else I'll scream for as long as it takes to get you where you belong - in jail!"

I shook my head, not so much in dismissal of her claim but rather in admiration at her cheek. And she was right. We weren't sadists - at least I wasn't.

"You're not a torturer, Mike," she said quietly. "And you can surely control your pet monkey, can't you?"

My pet monkey bared his teeth and growled.

"But I'll accept a third. We split the cash three ways. I won't settle for a penny less." She looked at me defiantly and I thought, why not, we can always amend things later on.

"How much have you got stashed away?" I asked. "I want paid in full, remember. At least!"

"You'll get your money," she sneered.

"What do you think, Heck?" I asked my partner. He shrugged. I think he was thinking what I had been thinking about breaking promises. "You're the boss," he said, but I didn't believe him.

"Right then, Natasha, it looks like you've got yourself a deal. Now. Which post office is it?"

She smiled and shook her head. "Tomorrow" she said. "We go together and do the split on the spot. "So," she continued coyly, "You'd better look after me tonight, Mike - you wouldn't want me to come to any harm, would you?"

I stared at her with embarrassment. Heck got the message too and he guffawed. "A' right then," he said. "Ah'll take the couch. At least that way ah'll get some sleep. Ye'll no' let her get away, will ye, Mike?"

I squirmed as Heck went to prepare to kip down and I followed Natasha into the bedroom. I closed the door and she took off her clothes and I took off mine and it was like old times. Until, exhausted by my exertions, I tried to snuggle under the clothes and sleep. Natasha had other plans. She nuzzled my ear and I groaned as I assumed that she wanted to go for the hat trick. She did, but not with me.

"Go see if your little pet wants to change places," she purred. "Please?"

The cheeky bitch! I was outraged of course, but what could I do? I rose from the bed, covered myself with a towel, grabbed my clothes and stomped out into the sitting room. When I woke Heck - he looked almost human when he was asleep - and told him of his command performance, I thought he was gong to decline. But he didn't - he must just have been groggy with sleep. A huge grin split his face and he bounded, naked, into the bedroom prepared already, I could see, to be of service. Disgusted, I stretched out on the couch and tried to get to sleep. Eventually to the accompaniment of bumps and giggles from next door, I did.

The next morning we took a taxi to Tottenham Court Road. London was looking bleak: rain lashed down and an east wind played keepy-uppy with yesterday's newspapers, discarded kebab containers and, I wouldn't be surprised, used condoms. Fortunately, colour was injected into the scene by regiments of golf umbrellas that bobbed along the pavements seeking negligent eyes to gouge. I felt happy because I was to be reunited with my money and Heck was happy because he was going to get some of it. I didn't know if Natasha was happy - after all, she was to be the loser - but she looked the happiest of all and I supposed it was because she was going to be rid of us soon and be available for someone else who would, presumably, give her more of what she craved.

We entered the post office at 9.35am. Natasha marched straight to the banks of metal lockers that lined one of the walls. With Heck and I guarding her shoulder (well, Heck protected her waist) she opened the box. Inside was a black attaché case. I made to take it but Natasha was too quick for me. She gripped it by the handle and yanked it from its steel enclosure.

"Somewhere public," she said out of the corner of her mouth. "Somewhere quiet but public. Or I'll start screaming now."

We retraced our steps out into the rain, an ordinary looking trio: an attractive woman flanked by her handsome (and younger) swain and her pet monkey.

"In here," the attractive woman hissed.

'Here' was a dingy-looking cafe which had the twin benefits of being empty and having individual booths with shoulder-high partition walls that afforded a fair amount of privacy. We sat in a middle compartment and ordered coffee from the waitress. When it came and she went Natasha opened the case.

"Oh!" said Heck.

"Ah!" said I.

The money was in hundred pound notes. Stacks of them. There must have been a million pounds worth.

"Three hundred thou," Natasha said.

"They're in bundles of twenty five thousand so take four each. Then bugger off."

Heck reacted first. He selected a bundle and riffled it to check that the bank notes went right to the bottom. Then he did the same with another three piles. Natasha and I looked on with a mixture of contempt and impatience. When it was my turn to be paid, I carelessly plucked four bundles from the case and tucked them away in my pockets.

"Well," I said.

Natasha's eyes flashed. She closed her case and made to rise. "Don't thank me," she said. "Just get out of my way."

I stood up and allowed her to pass into the aisle.

"You'll manage to pay for the coffees," she said and then she was gone.

I sat down again and looked at Heck, eyeball to eyeball across the table. For a minute we did not speak. Then, as one, we let out whoops of glee that brought the waitress to our table at a run.

"It's O.K." I told her. "We're just leaving. Here." I handed her a fiver. "For the coffee."

"Oh," she said. "I don't know if I've got

change yet . . . "

"So, keep it," I replied and, preceded by my trusty (and wealthy) pet monkey, left her stammering her thanks and wondering if Christmas had come early to London.

The capital had never looked lovelier. A double rainbow split the sky and, as we wandered into Piccadilly Circus, the fountain came on and its sparkling droplets of water created a haze that made the scene unreal. Mike and Hector in Wonderland: two lads, as happy as Larry, planning their retirements. We walked in silence until we came to the River Thames. We stood on the embankment and I thought that I might buy a boat and sail round the world. My crew would be all female and they would work topless. Heck whispered that he was going to buy a pub in Glasgow.

Upstream the Mother of Parliaments stood proud, secure, permanent. I recalled the meeting with Snyder and Mercouri at the Ritz where, for me, it had all begun. My heart beat wildly when I relived my coup at the Cardinal Casino and my conquest thereafter. That, of course, had ended unsatisfactorily and it had led me to go through with my mercenary training and subsequent mission in Uganda. I thought of the International Hotel and its nightclub on the roof; of the Tonton Macoutes and Makindye Prison and the underground cellar and the game of dominoes. I recalled the jail break, the interlude at the Rock Hotel and the safaris with satisfaction. Mombasa and the reckoning with Beresford had been the high point of the African adventure; catching up with Natasha in London had made it all worth while.

"Let's go home," I murmured to Heck. He nodded. "Aye," he said, "it's time tae get back."

****

My journey north was as sober as it was sad. I flew to Newcastle while Heck caught a train to Glasgow. We didn't exchange addresses because we didn't have addresses to exchange. We just shook hands and went our separate ways.

Heck had abandoned his plans to buy a pub and I of course would not be sailing round the world. Natasha's fault. The money, you see, that she had given us - every single banknote - was forged and, to add insult to injury, the forgery hadn't even been a very good one. We were lucky that the bookie who spotted the counterfeiting was an old buddy. He didn't take my bet of course – I hadn't been able to resist a flutter on 'Idi's Revenge' in the two o' clock at Newmarket. And it won, blast it. My other regret- admittedly slight – was knowing that I might have given Heck a parting gift : one that had been bequeathed to me, probably, by my little chum in Tororo. That it might have been channeled to him via Natasha would be little consolation to either of us.

The End